DEADLY WOODS II

A Deadly Terror Returns

DAVID CLOSE

 www.trafford.com

North America & international
toll-free: 1 888 232 4444 (USA & Canada)
fax: 812 355 4082

CONTENTS

Dedication

To all those who enjoy what Marsh's Bar has to offer!

PROLOGUE

The town of Marshton finally got back to a sense of normalcy after enduring many murders and acts of cannibalism brought upon the community by three notorious outlaws, two of whom died in a gun battle fought by local citizens, who brought the terrible terror in the woods to a bloody end. Two surviving outlaws remain in prison to this day. One, a woman who went by the name of Blow and also another person involved in the crimes was sentenced to life in prison for his part.

The woods surrounding the town of Marshton were now deemed to be safe after a mountain lion brought to the woods by the gang of outlaws was shot and killed by two local hunters who were attacked by the creature. The terror that haunted the woods appeared to be at an end.

Author's note

The town of Marshton, Pennsylvania is a fictional town created by the author. However, the fictional town could be any number of small towns located in the western part of the state.

CHAPTER 1

A Terror Appears

Alex Birch and his friend Sean Burns sat on Alex's patio drinking beers and enjoying the beautiful weather on Labor Day weekend. The temperature was pushing eighty degrees without a cloud in the sky. Alex was a former New York City teacher who had moved to Marshton in order to take over his parents' house, who had both recently passed away. Alex now taught European and American history at the local community college. Sean Burns was a New York City police detective on a month's vacation recovering from a gunshot wound in his leg. Alex and Sean had become good friends by playing on the same rugby team years ago and then as they both aged, they drank in the same city bar.

Alex invited Sean to Marshton to heal from his wound in a relaxed environment that Marshton offered, as compared to the city.

"So is the beer helping ease the pain?" Alex asked with a smile.

"Beer is nature's cure for almost any pain. You should know that from our rugby days," Sean replied.

"So how in the hell did you let yourself get shot? I thought you were smarter than that."

"I told you on the phone it was a fucking ricochet off the subway wall and it was beyond my control. Smarts had nothing to do with it. We got a tip by people in the subway station that two foreign men were acting really suspicious and my partner and I happened to be near the station. I went down one stairway nearest to them and my partner was going to go down another stairway behind them. However, I got down to face them and identified myself. I was about eight feet away from them when they instantly both started to pull out weapons. I shot both of them in their heads and they went down. One of their guns went off and hit the subway wall and then reflected into my leg. I was fucking lucky that those assholes didn't pull a wire and blow the whole station to pieces because they were wearing mucho explosives. My partner got there right after I brought them down and just shook his head when he saw all the explosives they had on. I'm glad they died right away and didn't have a second to pull on those damn wires.

"At least you got the pricks who were going to fire at you before they could set off the bombs strapped on their bodies. Now that was smart of you. You became a real, living hero, on all the media networks. You even were greeted by the governor in that big ceremony held at the mayor's office. I am proud of what you did my friend."

"I got this nice paid recovery time to spend in the hills with you. You do have a good deal here. Nice house, Nice, easy job. Nice bars, with nice people. Hell, you have it dicked here in nature's forgotten wilderness."

"I do like it here, but I miss the city in some ways. It can get pretty boring here at times."

"Boring isn't in my vocabulary in the city. That's for sure."

"I'm glad you were able to come up. Let's head down to the peaceful town of Marshton and enjoy some of the local bars."

"Good idea Alex. I'm all for it."

"You want to walk or ride? You are supposed to exercise that leg."

"Let's walk, as long as it's not too far. The leg is still pretty sore but I do need to exercise in order to get back into condition."

"It's only a couple of miles into town and we can cut through the park to avoid traffic."

"I wouldn't exactly classify the word traffic here as compared to the city's traffic."

"Would you like to call your wife before we head out?"

"She's visiting her parents in sunny Florida. Her law firm gave her a month's leave with pay, thanks to her brave police detective's heroics. I'll call her later." Sean said smiling.

"You are lucky that shot hit your leg and not your balls."

"I'll take luck as well as skill in my job."

"Don't let the medal you got go to your head. Now let's walk hero."

Both men finished their beer and got up. Alex and Sean were both nearing fifty years old and both men were in excellent condition, weighing around 190 lbs and over six feet tall. Sean had Irish red hair and freckles on his smooth face. His body was still quite firm. Alex had ash blond hair and a not quite as firm body as his friend. Both men still kept involved in sports such as tennis, golf and paddleball.

At the Marshton Golf Course the annual Labor Day weekend golf tournament was being held. Al Conner, the golf pro, started the play with a shotgun start. Dr. Lee Stone, Jody Stone, his wife and nurse, Karen Hecate, another of Dr. Stone's nurses and Dr. Ron Brown teed off on the fifth hole. Dr. Stone's team was one of the favorite's to win their flight due to the excellent talent of all four golfers. "Nice ball, right down the middle. Good start," Dr. Lee Stone said to Dr. Brown.

"If Jody hits her drive as she is capable of she will out drive me by twenty yards," Dr. Brown said to Dr. Stone.

The group went on to birdie the hole and moved on to the sixth tee, after Karen dropped in a six foot putt.

On a small, tree-lined trail a few miles from the Marshton Golf Course Don Boone Crockett drove his atv along the trail following what he thought were blood tracks, which he figured was from some animal that had been badly wounded. Don was an engineer who traveled all around the world for a company that did specialized work. His hometown was Marshton and he came back to town in between jobs.

His father had given him his middle name for he always thought Daniel Boone was a better frontiersman than Davy Crockett. Don constantly got his balls broken by his friends because of his middle name in regards to his last name. Don drove slowly down the trail looking toward the bloody tracks. He went around a turn in the trail when he stopped suddenly as he saw a human body hanging from a tree. The body skin had been half removed from the corpse! Don stared at the body hanging from a large elm tree by a rope that was around the victim's neck. He reached for his cell phone but there was no signal in this area of the woods. He knew that there were

4

several camps in this area, mostly owned by hunters from out of state. Most of the camps would be empty until deer season which didn't start for several months.

He thought of what he should do about the body hanging above his stare. It was hard to tell who it was as the skin had been removed from the upper body area. He saw that something was hanging out of the victim's mouth but before he got a closer look and could decide what to do, a shot rang out and hit the tree next to where he was standing. Don ducked behind his atv and he glanced in the direction of where he thought the shot had came from. Another shot hit in front of his atv. Don bent down and climbed on his atv and he drove it down a bank to the left side of the trail as another shot hit near the rear of the atv. He drove through a grove of saplings that barely had room for him to drive through, but at least he was covered from the directions the shots were coming from. He made his way away from where he found the hanging body. In Don's left hand he held a 357 pistol that he always carried with him in the woods. He turned and fired several shots in the general direction of where the shots were being fired at him. He wanted whoever was shooting at him to know that he was armed and ready to defend himself. He glanced back and then continued to drive away from the deadly scene, looking behind him as he drove but he was ready to shoot if he needed to. He had no idea who in the hell was firing at him or why. He knew he needed to get to an area where his cell phone could get a signal and fast.

Back at the Marshton Golf Course, Dr. Lee Stone hit his second shot on the par five, ten feet from the hole. "Nice shot Lee," Jody said as she gave her husband a hug.

Dr. Brown added, "That will give us a real chance at an eagle putt."

The eagle putt was made by Dr. Brown and after that shot the team was seven under par. As the team prepared to tee off on their next hole of play, wild excitement and yelling happened with the foursome in front of them. "What is going on up ahead of us. What'd they do hole out on a shot or something?" Karen asked.

Dr. Stone put his yardage finder up to his eye and quickly said, "They are being attacked by animals. Quick, let's get up there to help!"

Three coyotes were attacking the foursome ahead of Dr. Stone's group. Mike Bombfield had been bitten on the arm. Cody Wayne was spraying his beer into the face of a coyote in an attempt to keep him away from Rich Montana who was moving around the golf cart trying to avoid the snarling animals. Jeff Bayern was swinging a three wood at an attacking coyote who was ignoring the hits to his body. When Dr. Stone's group arrived they too started swinging clubs at the animals in an attempt to drive them away. Finally the animals retreated into the woods where the dogleg turned to the left. Dr. Stone treated Bombfield's arm to stop the bleeding. Cody Wayne said, "I've never seen anything like that. Coyotes are usually afraid of people. They just wouldn't quit."

"It's lucky that no one else was hurt by them. Those bastards were trying to kill us," Jeff Bayern said.

"I wonder if they liked the beer that you soaked that one with Cody?" said Rich Montana. Cody Wayne just smiled and shook his head.

"We better get Mike to the hospital and let Al Conner know what happened out here. So much for the tournament.

We can't continue with the coyotes on the prowl. They could attack again some place else on the course," Dr. Stone added.

"What in hell did you do to make them attack you?" Dr. Brown asked.

Bayern answered, "We didn't do a damn thing. They just came running at us from the woods."

The two foursomes got in their carts and drove toward the clubhouse.

Don Boone Crockett drove back onto the trail he came down and sped as fast as he could handle his atv on the wood-lined small trail.

He made it to a larger trail that led to a small tavern called JK's. Don hurried inside and used the land line phone to call the Norm Smithson, the Marshton Town police chief. The chief, after hearing about the dead body and the shots being fired at Don, immediately called the state police and spoke to Captain Mark Mason. It was agreed that Norm Smithson would meet Don Boone Crockett at JK's Tavern while Captain Mason and several troopers would go to where the dead body was located according to the location given by Crockett. Before Chief Smithson left his office he answered a call from the Marshton Golf Pro, Al Conner, who related to the chief about the coyote attack. The chief then called Ben Wooly, the local game warden and advised him to go to the golf course and check out the situation. The chief also asked his deputy Tom Rogers to go up to the golf course to get a first hand report on what took place during the coyote attack. The chief then left to hear what information Crockett could give him about the dead body and the shots fired at him. "This is going to be one hell of a long day," the chief thought to himself as he started his car.

Alex Birch and Sean Burns walked down to an Italian establishment called Albelli's, which was known for its great Italian entrees and wide selection of beer and wine. Alex introduced Sean to the owners, Carla, and George Albelli then ordered two Harp beers. Alex knew from past experience that his friend was a big fan of Harp beer and this was the place in town that carried the Irish brand. The alcohol content was high, which was also a plus. Both men clinked their bottles together when the beers arrived at the bar. "Here's to a real hero and the quick healing of your leg," Alex said as he pointed at his friend's leg.

Carla asked Sean, "Didn't I see you on a TV news broadcast recently from New York City?"

Alex answered for Sean, "You did Carla. This is a real, live hero who stopped a terrorist attack."

Sean just shook his head at Alex and Carla put two more beers on the bar and said, "The beers are on us and thanks for your actions."

"Thank you Carla and George, the Harp beer will certainly aid in my healing." The men had one more beer each and then said goodbye to the Albellis and left. Their next stop was on the way home, a bar called The Marsh. The bar was a working person's bar and was nearly one hundred years old and one of Alex's favorite places to stop when he walked into town. The conversation in the bar was all about the coyote attack at the local golf course today. Alex and Sean sat down at a table with two men Alex knew from his frequent stops at The Marsh and he introduced Sean to Art Fisher and Jim Sparta.

Art said, "So did you hear about the golf course attack by coyotes today?"

Sparta added, "The owner of this bar and several of his pals were the ones who were attacked. One guy, Mike Bombfield, known in here as Bomber, got bitten on his arm by one of the coyotes."

"Does this kind of thing happen around here a lot?" Sean asked the men.

"Sean's from New York City and only deals with two legged animals," Alex said.

Fisher stated, "I've never heard of a group of coyotes attacking anybody. I wonder if Bomber will have to get rabies shots?"

"Maybe the golfers around here will have to carry an extra club called a 357," Jim Sparta said with a grin.

A man named Hoss at the bar said, "Those coyotes can get real mean if provoked or cornered. Bomber is lucky he only got bit on the arm."

Alex ordered another round of drinks for the table and the bar conversation continued about the now infamous coyote attack.

At JK's Tavern Chief Smithson sat with Don Crockett who told him the events that happened from the time he entered the trail, to finding the hanging body, to being shot at and finally to making his escape. Then the chief walked with Don outside to look at the bullet hole in front of Don's atv. The chief said, "We are going to need that bullet out of your atv. Mind if I get it now so we won't need to haul your atv into town. I'm sure the state boys will need to compare this one with the ones they might find around where the shots were fired at you."

Don looked at his damaged atv and said, "Sure get it now. I think it's probably still in there somewhere. I'll help you look for it. I'm just glad it's not inside of me. There's a bullet hole in the back too."

The two men found the bullet that was lodged into the floor and also the one from the rear of the atv. They appeared to be from a high powered rifle. The chief then said, "I'm going to go up to where you said the body was located. How about coming with me because I'm sure the troopers will have a shit load of questions for you so you might just as well get it over with now. When I called them they told me they wanted to speak with you as soon as possible."

"Fine, I'll pick the atv when we are done up there. I'll tell you Norm that was freaking crazy up there when the shots were coming at me. Who in the hell would do that?"

"I have no idea but let's get back up there and talk to the troopers."

At the Marshton Hospital Mike Bombfield had the bite on his arm treated by a very pretty doctor named Dr. Danielle Steelman, who was talking in the hallway near the emergency room. "Unless the coyote that bit Mike is tested he'll need rabies shots," Dr. Steelman said.

Dr. Brown replied, "There is no way to know which coyote had bitten Mike. I think he's going to need the shots unless the antibiotics can be trusted have the wound purified."

"The wound wasn't that deep and I cleaned it the best I could with what was available at the golf course. We better put the choice up to him. Those shots are quite painful, even with today's improvements," Dr. Stone added.

Ben Wooly arrived at the golf course and learned the that coyotes had returned to the woods surrounding the course. He then asked for volunteers to track the coyotes after making sure that anyone going with him had weapons in case they were also attacked. Wooly waited at the course for several men to go and get weapons. Thirty minutes later the hunt for the coyotes had started. Wooly did give the permission to shoot on site any coyote that they located. Deputy Rogers led one group of men and Wooly led another group into the area where the coyotes had gone after the attack.

A man named Sprout entered The Marsh and said in a loud voice, "I was at JK's Tavern and Boone came in, (Don Crockett's friends either called him Boone or Crockett) and said that he found a dead body hanging from a tree and then was shot at by some asshole. It happened near the golf course."

"What the hell are you talking about? There was a coyote attack on the golf course. No one said anything about a dead body," Jim Edwin said in a questioning voice.

"I'm telling you I heard it right from Boone. Chief Smithson was there and I saw the bullet holes in Boone's atv. It's real and happened just a short while ago," Sprout said in a defensive manner.

Alex Birch looked at Sean Burns and said, "Did you hear that? That's hard to grasp. Murders don't happen around here."

"It appears that they do. Nice relaxing place to recover. Animal attacks and now a dead body and shots going off in your woods. I can't wait until my wife asks me how relaxing the environment is up here?"

Cody Wayne walked into his bar with Jeff Bayern and Rich Montana. Cody said, "Give everyone a drink. I know I need one after the golf experience." Judy, who was tending bar, gave everyone in the bar the standard chip . . . a camo-colored pen.

"Just wait until you hear what Sprout told us. Tell them," Edwin said.

Sprout repeated the story of what happened to Boone near the golf course.

Art Fisher looked at Jim Sparta and said, "What in fuck's sake is going on out there today? I'm glad I don't golf."

"A good day to be in The Marsh where it's nice and safe," Sparta said.

Alex and Sean said their goodbyes and began their walk home.

When Chief Smithson and Don Crockett arrived at the crime scene the state troopers had crime scene tape around a wide area near the dead body which was still hanging from a tree while pictures were being taken. Some troopers were looking at trees to see if any bullets could be discovered and other troopers were using metal detectors. Captain Mark Mason came up to Cheif Smithson and said, "I assume this is the person who discovered the body and was shot at by the suspect who is now in the wind."

The chief answered, "Yes, Captain Mason this is Don Crockett who is the man who came down the trail on his atv and after he found the body in the tree several shots were fired at him. A couple shots hit his atv and I have the bullets in an evidence bag. I saw the atv and removed the bullets myself."

"We found a couple of bullets in some nearby trees but they were, it looked like, from a pistol and not a rifle."

Crockett said, "I fired in the direction of where the shots were being fired at me; mainly so the bastard doing the shooting would know that I was armed. I was in one damn hurry to get away from here alive."

"Look Captain, I know Don and you can believe what he is telling you as the honest truth."

"I'm not doubting him. It is, just as you well know, that we have to cover all the bases. I had to know where the pistol shots came from."

Two crime scene techs dropped the body slowly down from the tree and Don Crockett glanced down at the body on the ground and said,

"I didn't know his penis had been cut off!"

Mason said, "You didn't see that when you were here before?"

"No I didn't. Just when I looked up at the body shots began flying at me and I ducked and was lucky enough that none hit me."

"Why in hell is the skin peeled from the upper body? It looks like a scaling knife must have been used. Damn! Is there any indication of who the victim might be?" The chief asked.

Mason answered, "No idea who the vic is. No identification was to be seen anywhere around."

"There has to be one sick individual out there some place. What is your plan to find the sicko?" the chief asked.

"We are in the process of searching the surrounding area as we speak. Whoever did this didn't leave much in the way of clues. The media is going to be all over this soon and Don it would help if you didn't answer too much other then you found the body and got out."

"Sure I will do that. I really didn't see much with the shots coming at me."

"I'm going to take Don back to get his atv and I have to let the mayor know what is happening because she will have to face the media as well as us."

Captain Mason nodded and said, "I'll be in touch later so we can coordinate a plan of attack to get this killer. Talk to you later."

On the ride back to JK's Tavern Chief Smithson asked Crockett to stop down at his office and fill out a witness report later today and also asked him to avoid saying much about what he saw at the crime scene.

Crockett agreed to do both. Cheif Smithson got a call from deputy Rogers on the way back to town. He was told that the search for the coyotes only turned up a fox that had been ripped to pieces and there was coyote hair all around the dead fox but no sign of the coyotes.

Penny Sullivan, the new editor of the local paper, took a call at home from a friend who told her about the coyote attack on the golf course and also there was talk at the golf course that a dead body had been found in the woods near the golf course. Penny thanked her friend and then called her primary reporter, Melissa Travers. Sullivan told her reporter the news that had been related to her by a source. Melissa was asked to go up to the golf course and gather what information she could about the coyote attack. Penny ended the call and thought about the report of a dead body in the woods. She called the police station but was stonewalled as to any report of a dead body. She decided to drive out to the area around the golf course and see what was happening.

CHAPTER 2

No Clear Answers

Chief Smithson arrived at the station and immediately called Darlene La Clare, Mayor of Marshton, in order to inform her of both the murder in the woods and the coyote attack on the golf course. Mayor La Clare questioned the chief on what facts he knew for certain.

The police chief told her that the body was hanging from a tree and skin was missing from the body, like it was scaled off with a knife. Also that the man's penis had been cut off. At this point there has been no identification of the victim. Also the blood pool below the body was relatively fresh. Don Crockett found the body and someone fired shots at him; probably it was the killer who fired the shots. The state police are now on the scene. The mayor said that she wanted to be kept informed of any developments and would be talking with the state police soon.

Back at the crime scene in the woods the state police medical examiner had arrived and the victim was ready to be removed to the crime lab. Captain Mason asked Ted Williams, the medical examiner, if he thought that this was some type of weird sex crime and Williams stated that he thought that it well could be judging from the removal of the man's penis and layers of skin from the body. It had grown dark and the portable lighting around the scene cast dark shadows in all directions. The troopers were unable to find any tracks of a shooter nor were any spent shells found.

Penny Sullivan could see the portable lights from the road where she had parked her car. She got out of the car and a trooper approached her and said, "Sorry lady but you can't go up in the woods. This is a crime scene."

"Look I am with the local paper and I have press credentials."

"I'm sorry but you still can't approach the crime scene."

"Who is in charge here? I'd like to speak to that person."

"Captain Mason is the ranking officer and I'm sure he is quite busy at the crime scene."

"Look, I have heard about the dead body found up there so don't try to say that there isn't information that the public is entitled to know. I want to speak to your Captain Mason."

The trooper called on a radio to reach Captain Mason. The captain's voice came on the radio and said, "There will be a press release in due time. Right now this is an active crime scene and details are too sketchy to be released before we have more complete information."

Penny Sullivan shook her head and said, "Tell your captain that I'll be in touch with him for the details that he seems fit to keep from the press." She then walked back to her car and drove away. The trooper flipped a finger at the back of her car as it left.

Melissa Travers had interviewed several people at the golf course and also the men who had went on a search for the coyotes involved in the attack on the course. She did find out that a mulilated dead fox had been found and it was suspected that the coyotes had killed it. She also got the names of the golfers who were attacked from Al Conner, the golf pro. She planned to stop at The Marsh bar to see if the owner, Cody Wayne, was there to interview him, since he was one of the golfers who had been attacked.

Alex and Sean were outside of Alex's house around the fire pit in his yard. Sean Burns was talking to his wife Jessica on his smart phone.

"Yes it is relaxing up here. No constant noise from taxis, or subways and sirens echoing. However, there was a coyote attack on a local golf course today and oh yeah there was a murder in the woods today. Relaxing as hell around here."

"Are you serious? A murder up there in God's country and some kind of animal attack too. I hope you have your gun with you if that's what is going on there," Jessica said with a serious tone.

"I'm not involved in any of it. Alex has a nice safe location far from where the dead body was found. So I really can relax around here. I hope you are getting nice and tan down there in the sunshine. Say hello to your parents. See you soon. Love you."

"Love you too. Be careful up there."

"Isn't love grand? Jesse's a great wife Sean. You are one lucky detective. Let's go inside and check out the Yankee game."

Melissa Travers gave the information she had collected at the golf course to Penny Sullivan by way of her smart phone and she told her editor that she was going to stop by The Marsh in an attempt to get more info from the golfers who were attacked. Melissa pulled in the parking lot behind the small bar and went inside. There were several people at the bar who glanced in her direction. She looked around the bar and asked, "Is the owner here? I'm Melissa Travers from the Marshton paper. I'd like some information on what happened at the golf course today."

"I'm the owner, Cody Wayne, and I was playing golf today. I didn't expect to be attacked by coyotes but that was what happened."

"I heard one person in your group was bitten and he was the only one hurt. Is that true?"

"Yeah, Bomber was bitten on the arm. We were lucky those crazy coyotes didn't get to more of us," Cody said.

Jeff Bayern added, "Cody sprayed beer on the face of one coyote attacking us. I guess the creature didn't like Miller beer cause he ran back into the woods."

Melissa smiled and said, "Why did they come after you in the first place? Did you have food they wanted?"

"We had plenty of beer. Maybe they were alcoholic coyotes," Rich Montana said laughing.

Laura Wayne, who was tending bar asked, "Can I get you a drink?"

"No thank you I have to get back to the office. I'm glad you are all safe and thank you for talking with me." Melissa then left the bar.

Chief Smithson was on the phone with Captain Mason, who filled him in on all the information he and his crime scene team had recovered from the scene. Tomorrow the troopers would be going to all the cabins near the crime scene to talk to anyone who might live or be staying in the cabins. Basically, Mason told the chief that there were no clues as to why or who did the killing. Hopefully DNA testing might help identify the victim but that will take some time even with the rush Mason had put on it with the ME. Chief Smithson put the phone down and started to make a list of things which he would talk over with Mayor La Clare tomorrow. The chief had already told Penny Sullivan that he had no comment on either of the events which happened today; both at the golf course or the murder in the woods. Sullivan wasn't happy about the chief's "no comment" statement and said she would get back to him after she spoke to the mayor.

Penny Sullivan and Melissa Travers worked together on the story that would be in the morning paper. The information they had was just the basic info that they were able to pry out of people and the state police. Local police chief gave no information.

Murder . . . Mystery . . . and Mayhem

Sullivan and Travers: Once again the woods around Marshton have been the scene of what officials as of yet cannot explain or won't explain. What we do know is that a dead body has been found in the woods near the local golf course and that a coyote attack has occurred on the golf course leaving one man injured, Mike Bombfield, who was bitten in the arm. State Police Captain Mark Mason refused to give any details on the murder or identify the victim. Chief Smithson simply said, "No comment." Mason did promise a press briefing in the near future. Meanwhile we will be searching for answers to who the dead body is and why the coyotes suddenly attacked golfers.

The newspaper article went on to print several witness statements and to state that the public is entitled for more information as a killer remains at large and dangerous coyotes are roaming the area woods.

Both Captain Mark Mason and Chief Smithson agreed to let Don Crockett leave town the next day for an important job his company had scheduled in Mexico to repair a factory that couldn't open until it had been repaired and Crockett had the ability to do the repairs. He had given a written witness statement and both Mason and Smithson felt it was a good thing to get him away from the questions the press would ask him when they found out he saw the body and what had been done to it. They knew where he would be located at and could reach him if they needed to. So Crockett was permitted to go to the job that awaited him.

When the morning paper reached the citizens of Marshton, the town was in shock at what had happened in the area surrounding their town.

No one knew who had been killed in the woods or why coyotes had attacked golfers. The Marsh bar was packed with people who wanted to hear from Cody Wayne what had happened on the golf course. The phone at the police station constantly rang, and the "No Comment" reply was the answer given to all callers. The Marshton paper's phone also rang continually and the answer given to callers was, "We will be out digging for more answers today." The Marshton golf course was closed and another search was going to be conducted for coyotes in the near-by woods by several local people who were normally deer hunters and knew their way around wooded areas.

Alex Birch handed the morning paper to Sean Burns, who said, "That headline will attract everyone's attention. That's for sure. I don't envy the police chief or the state police because they are going to be bombarded with questions they really can't or don't want to answer."

"How would you investigate this if you were in charge? I mean what would you do to find the killer? There doesn't seem to be a lot of information out there."

"There's always information out there no matter if it seems there isn't any. The ME might be able to provide clues after checking out the body. The crime scene techs could come up with some small bit of info to see if the killer is in the police data base or even the victim. As an investigator you take what's there and turn it into something. Most cases are solved by doing what Doyle's Sherlock Holmes did, by using good old deductive reasoning. Believe me the clues are there it's just a matter of locating them."

"Well it will be interesting once more details are known from the investigation."

"Yes it certainly will."

In the mayor's office Chief Smithson said, "I really don't think we want the public to know how grusome the victim was left. I mean you want people to know the he had skin peeled from the body and his penis was cut off like I mentioned to you before? I think we have to keep some details private as long as we can."

"We are going to be asked for information from Penny Sullivan and who knows what other papers may pick up on what happend. Norm, we have to be ready to release what we know."

"We can push it off to the state police to release information to the press. I'm sure they want everything released to go through them and not us."

"It can come back on us that we knew information but didn't give it to the citizens. Think about that."

"Darlene, the state police have more information than we do. They processed the crime scene after all. We direct questions we get over to them. That's what they would want us to do. Captain Mason is a good guy and knows what he is doing. We are going to coordinate the investigation and he will share information with us as long as we play it the way he wants us to. He did make that clear to me when we spoke on the phone.

"Ok Norm. Penny Sullivan isn't going to be happy. I have a meeting with her in an hour and she's going to press me for what we know. I can direct her to you and you can direct her to Captain Mason."

"That's the way to go. Direct her to me on answers you don't want to get out. That's the safe way to keep us in the loop with the state police."

Captain Mason was talking with the ME, who was explaining what he had found in the processing of the body. The ME said, "The vic had no wounds except a small penetration to his heart, which was the death wound. He quickly bled out. His facial skin was cut off either before he died or after. I can't tell which. However, there was definately meth in the man's system so either he was a user or someone put it into his system. In either case meth was involved in the crime."

"Perhaps the killer was on meth in order to do what happened to the victim. Any news on how long the DNA will take to get back?"

"I sent the DNA to the Pittsburgh lab for faster results. I'll let you know just as soon as I hear anything."

"Ok, thanks again. Perhaps we are dealing with some meth heads in the woods. That makes things more nuts for all of us."

Penny Sullivan was totally disgusted after her meeting with both the mayor and the chief of police as she had kept being directed to Captain Mason of the state police for answers to her questions. She knew that Melissa Travers had been to The Marsh and that information pertained to the coyote attack, but Penny was more interested in the murder investigation and what questions that were not being answered by anyone involved. The editor decided to drive out to JK's Tavern, where a great many people who knew the woods frequented. When she arrived at the tavern and walked inside. The bartender was the owner JK. Penny sat at the bar where two other customers sat. "I'm Penny Sullivan from the Marshton paper. I have some questions that you can help me with."

JK smiled and said, "I know who you are so ask away."

"I'm sure you have heard or read about that murder in the woods. Do you happen to know any details about it that some of your customers may have related to you. I'm looking for more information then the police or state police are willing to share and I feel that people are entitled to know more about it."

"Well I heard from a man who actually found the body. He came here right after he found the body and was shot at by someone near the body."

Penny Sullivan was busy taking notes as JK spoke. She looked up and asked, "Who was the man who found the body? I sure would like to talk to him about it."

"He's a friend of mine, Boone, is what I call him, but his name is Don Crockett. He can't talk to you about it because he left for Mexico on an important job for his company. He's a top class engineer."

"So he's gone and he's a witness. That doesn't make sense."

"I'm just telling you what I know and I know he's gone."

"Did he tell you anything about what he saw?"

"It wasn't a pretty scene up there. The body was hanging from a tree and his private part was cut off. Plus Boone was shot at. His atv was hit by some bullets.

Penny shook JK's hand and said, "You have been more helpful than anyone in authority. Thank you so very much."

"My pleasure."

Penny left the tavern and sat in her car processing what she had just learned from JK.

The men searching for the coyotes at the golf course were several hundred yards into the woods when Ben Wooly, the game warden stopped to stare down at the two dead coyotes on the ground or what was left of them. They had been torn to pieces. Kraig Kalhoon, a well known hunter in the area stood next to Ben Wooly and pointed at animal tracks on the ground. "Those are definitely bear tracks. This is strange. Coyotes don't normally mess with bears and bears don't attack most any animal. It sure looks like a bear has killed these coyotes for some reason."

"What a mess. We need to get these remains out of here so they can be tested for rabies. Remember the guy had been bitten by a coyote. I'll send back for some body bags."

"None of this makes any sense. First the attack on the golf course and now a bear fighting coyotes," Kraig stated.

"Well we gotta take them back."

Captain Mason said to trooper at the desk, "Did those search warrants get signed yet? We have a bunch of cabins to check out today.

If we need authorization for overtime I'll approve it in advance."

"The warrants have been approved. So we are taking automatic weapons with us to check on the cabins?" The trooper asked.

"You're damn right we are taking automatics with us. Who knows what we may find in those cabins? Better to be prepared for the worst case senario. There's a real nut out there," Mason answered.

CHAPTER 3

A Bloody Scene

Dr. Stone was meeting with Mike Bombfield in his office. "You made the correct choice about having the preventive shots just in case you were exposed to rabies by the coyote that had bitten you. You have already been given the immune globulin shot and now you need four more shots over a fourteen day period."

"I heard you have to get the shots in the stomach," Bombfield said with caution.

"That was once the case but now you get the shots in the arm and my two nurses are experts at giving shots."

"I'm not a fan of getting any shots Doc."

"It won't hurt and you'll get a piece of candy after the shot if you'd like, just like any child who gets a shot."

"I'd much rather have a beer, if you don't mind."

Nurse Jody came into the room with a prepared shot. "Which arm do you want me to give you the shot Mr. Bombfield?"

"I'm right-handed so in my left. I'm not going to look when you do it."

Jody gave Mike the shot and the other nurse Karen, entered the room and handed Mike a big lollypop."

"See you soon for yet another shot Mike," Dr. Stone said.

"Right and I'm so looking forward to it," Mike said as he looked at his left arm.

Ron Macintire was driving down North Road a few miles from the golf course when a large black bear came out of the woods and intentionally ran into Macintire's jeep. The jeep spun and came to a stop. The bear clawed at the front window and then rambled off into the woods. Ron sat in amazement and watched the bear leave the scene.

After a short time he got out of his jeep and inspected the damage. There was a large dent in the side where the bear struck and the driver's side window was cracked from the bear's clawing. Macintire said to himself, "What in hell was that all about? It was like the bear attacked my jeep on purpose and then just left."

Most of the cabins the troopers were searching were empty because the majority of cabins were owned by out-of-town hunters who would not be coming to the area until deer season, which was months away. Two troopers walked onto the porch of a cabin located a few miles from where the dead body had been found. Trooper Jones knocked on the door and a man answered wearing just shorts. Trooper Jones said, "We have a warrant to search your cabin."

"What for?" the man asked.

"There has been a murder a few miles from your location and we are searching all the cabins in the area and also to warn persons of the danger they may be in."

"I'm from Buffalo, New York and came down to relax for a few days," the man in the cabin said. A woman came out of the bedroom and looked at the trooper standing in the door.

"What's wrong John?"

"They have a warrant to search the cabin. There's been a murder near here."

"Sir, what is your name?" Trooper Jones asked.

"My name is John Simpson and this is my girlfriend Jean."

"Are you the owner of this cabin?" Jones asked.

"Yes I am. I usually come down in hunting season but like I said we decided to come down for this long weekend."

"We won't bother you but we need to take a quick look around. By the way this is my partner, Robert Cutcher."

"Ok help yourself," Simpson said.

The two troopers walked through the cabin and saw nothing out of order. There was a bottle of wine on the kitchen table and some beer in the fridge. No sign of drugs or anything illegal. Before leaving Trooper Jones said, "You need to be aware of any strangers about. We have a very dangerous person around who has killed one person. Have you seen any strangers around?"

"Not that I have noticed," Simpson replied.

"Well be careful and thanks for your time," Jones said. The troopers then left the cabin.

John Simpson said to his girlfriend, "I think we'll pack and head back to Buffalo. This sounds a bit too risky to stay any longer."

Trooper Jones and Cutcher began walking through the woods on their way to the next cabin. Cutcher said, "Lucky we have that map marking where all the cabins near here are located."

Jones stated, "I feel like I'm in a jungle where some creature could jump at us any second."

"I know what you mean," Cutcher said.

Penny Sullivan and Melissa Travers were busy compiling information for tomorrow's paper. "If Captain Mason doesn't respond to my call for a comment on the information I got at JK's Tavern, then we will go without his comment."

"What about the new information about the two coyotes that were found dead near the golf course. It appears they were killed by a bear according to what I was told by Ben Wooly,"

"We have to combine it in with the story about the dead body and now we know the main witness is out of the country and that shots were fired at him when he discovered the body. I think we leave out that the victim's penis was cut off and some of his skin was removed."

"The state police must have information they aren't letting out. I'm giving Mason another half hour and I'm calling him again."

In Mayor La Clare's office Chief Smithson said, "We have a killer on the loose, who is quite crazy judging what he did to the victim and we have coyotes going nuts on the golf course, plus school is opening in another few days."

"I have been thinking about that. There are a great many children who live in the townships and would have to wait outside for their bus.

I don't like it," Mayor La Clare said. "I've been thinking we need the school superintendent involved. I'm calling him right now." The mayor placed a call to Dr. Bruce Murphy's home phone and only got a voice message. "That sucks. Not home. I left a message for him to contact me as soon as possible."

"He might be out of town and might not be back until tomorrow. Don't you have his cell phone number? The chief asked.

"I don't but I'll get it when he calls."

"So what do we do now?"

"I call the Assistant Super, Anne Jackson."

Captain Mason got a call from the ME and was told that the victim had been identified as Thomas Blackburn, who was in the data base. He was arrested for drug possession two years ago. The drugs he had on him were meth and some pot. He had just been released a month ago.

"Thanks for the quick work. Do we know where he was from?"

"How's all around? Nothing stable. He was arrested in Cleveland, Ohio. I'll contact them and see what they have on him or anyone related to him."

"Good and thanks again." Mason said and realized that meth was a big factor in the vic's recent life anyway. Now to find out who the vic was associated with. Mason asnwered his phone. It was Penny Sullivan from the Marshton Paper. "What can I do for you Miss Sullivan?"

"Well you can start by being honest and clear with me"

"What exactly do you mean by that?"

"Come on Captain Mason. I know about who found the body. I know about the shots that were fired. I know the person that found the body is now out of the country on a job. I know the victim was tortured by having skin and his penis removed. How's that for openers?"

"Well, well, it seems you have been quite busy. How did you get your information?"

"Now I can't give you my source, you know that. Now before the paper comes out tomorrow would you care to comment?"

"I cannot comment on the ongoing investigation. You know that."

"So you are not denying any of the facts I mentioned?"

"I do wish you would consider not publishing those facts you mentioned. By doing so you could make the investigation more difficult."

"It happens to be my duty to inform the public so they can be aware of the danger that is still out there."

"It's my duty, as you say, not to compromise the investigation."

"So you still have no comment?"

"That's correct. Now I have a lot to do right now. Goodbye Miss Sullivan," Mason ended the conversation.

Penny looked at Melissa and said, "He didn't deny what I told him so we go with his, "No Comment," and write our story."

Alex Birch and Sean Burns drove down to Abelli's to have a late dinner of fine Italian food. The place was crowded and they sat down at the one open table in the far corner. Both men ordered Harp beers from the waitress, who was named Laurie and she said hello to Alex. "So when is Jesse coming to Marshton?" Alex asked his friend.

"I guess in about a week, then we are going to Niagara Falls. Neither of us have ever been there and I thought as long as we are this close, why not go."

"I've seen it many times. You can gamble in the casino up there now.

"That's good to know. Just how long can you watch water fall down?"

"Well it will be a nice change of pace for you both," Alex said as he looked at a man who waved at him from the bar. "Hello Pitt, how goes it?" The man named Pitt gave Alex a thumbs up sign.

"What did you call that guy?" Sean asked.

"His name is Dan Augustin, but everyone calls him Pitt because he is a Pittsburgh Steelers fan, a Pirates fan, a Penguins fan and a Pittsburgh Panther fan. So the name he is called is simply Pitt because of all the Pittsburgh teams he likes."

"I guess that makes sorta sense," Sean said with a grin.

"Let's order. I'm starved. The cooks are really special in here the chef is named Deano and his assistant is Valerine." Sean ordered lasagne and Alex ordered rigatoni. Over dinner the men discussed the Yankees and the murder investigation going on in Marshton.

Penny Sullivan and Melissa Travers finally finished the front page story for tomorrow's paper.

Terror Returns To Our Woods

Sullivan—Travers: Terror has once again appeared in our area woods in the form of murder and unprovoked animal attacks. Two days ago a dead body had been discovered by a local resident. The body was hanging from a tree and torture had been done to the victim, who as of yet has not been identified. Whover killed the victim is still at large so citizens need to be aware and very careful. Gun shots were fired at the resident who discovered the body. The state police are presently conducting the investigation with the help of local police. Citizens should notify police of any strangers near their homes.

To make matters even worse, animal attacks happened at the golf course as this paper reported and as of late, information came to us of two dead coyotes killed by a bear near the golf course. Again, caution is advised by all persons in all ways.

Captain Mason, of the state police, when asked to comment about the occurrences in our woods simply said, "No comment at this time." Also, Chief Smithson was asked to comment about the new information obtained by this paper and he too had no comment and referred us to the state police for comment.

(The remainder of the article contained interviews with local residents about the murder and about the animal attacks on the golf course.)

Mayor La Clare finally got a call from Dr. Bruce Murphy, who had been contacted by his Assistant Superintendent Anne Jackson. "I've been informed of the terrible news of the murder in the woods and of the coyote attacks on the golf course. Do you really think that the entire school district should be closed? That would be a real burden on the parents of this community."

"Well superintendent, it would be a bigger burden on the parents if a child is confronted by a crazed killer at large or attacked by animals that could be rabid. Don't you think so?" the mayor stated.

"I do see your point Mayor La Clare. Let me contact some board members and I'll get back to you. I'll be back in town tomorrow," Murphy then ended the call.

Darlene La Clare said out loud, "I just hope nothing else occurs in those woods."

Troopers Jones and Cutcher had only a few more cabins to check out and darkness was starting to close-in over the woods. Jones turned to Cutcher and said, "Let's do the cabin that is deeper in the woods first and then do the one that is closer to North Road so we can radio for a ride back."

"Sounds good John," Cutcher replied. The two troopers walked over a steep incline and saw a cabin. There was a Ford truck parked in front of the cabin. "Looks like we have someone home."

Jones said, "Let's approach this place with caution. Our killer could be inside." Both men moved slowly down to the cabin. As they neared the cabin they could see that a window had been pried open. Both men drew their weapons and went up on the porch. They could see that the door was ajar. Jones called inside, "We are the state police and we are coming in."

A woman's voice from the rear of the cabin called out, "Please help me." Jones glanced at Cutcher and both men entered the cabin with their guns pointed to the front of them. The troopers didn't see any person in the living area or the small kitchen.

"You check that bedroom and I'll check the other one," Jones said to Cutcher.

Cutcher heard a woman's voice inside the bedroom he neared, "Help, please help me."

Cutcher opened the door and to his shock saw a naked woman on the bed with both of her hands tied to the bed posts. "John, in here," Cutcher yelled.

Jones joined Cutcher in the bedroom and they went to the bed to free the woman's hands. She cried out, "He tied me here and raped me. He took my husband outside."

"What's you name?" Jones asked.

"I'm Mrs. Jane Wilson and my husband Dennis and I own this camp. A crazy man broke inside and did this to me and took Dennis out back. Will you see if he is ok?"

"Get dressed Mrs. Wilson and we will check on your husband," Cutcher told her. Both troopers walked toward the back door and Cutcher asked Jones, "Should we radio this in now for some back-up?"

"Let's check on the husband first." The men walked out of the door and immediately saw a man who had been nailed to a tree. He was naked and his penis had been removed and placed in his mouth! Both troopers looked at the man and then at each other. "What in the fuck is going on around here?" Jones said.

Just then a man stepped from behind a tree and raised his arms up. "I think you dudes must be searching for me. Isn't that right?"

Both troopers pointed their weapons at the man. Jones said, "Don't mov . . . ."

Suddenly, a naked woman emerged from the cabin, smiling with a glock pistol in her hands. She fired at the troopers hitting both of the men in their backs. They both fell forward on the ground. The naked woman went to them and shot one round into each of their heads. "Chalk up two state boys," The man, known as Willy, said as he walked over to the woman and kissed her.

"Your plan worked perfect. Fixing my wrists to the bed fooled them completely. What a bunch of damn fools. Lucky you saw them in the woods. Now we better split the scene before they come looking for these two dead ones. Better clean sweep the place first." the woman, who was called Kite said. (since her school days was always high as a kite)

"Who did you tell them you were?" the Willy asked.

"Why I am Mrs. Wilson and whoever that is nailed to the tree is my husband, Mr. Wilson. They bought the story. Do I have time to fuck with them like the guy on the tree?"

"Baby I'd like to fuck you right now, right here but you're right we need to hit the road if we plan to continue with our adventure. We better get up to the guy's atv we hid up the hill after we do a check on the inside. They might have roadblocks set up and those two dead troopers might have called the guy's truck's plate in," Willy said.

"Can't we get high first?" the Kite asked.

"That we can do," Willy said.

"You know that the guy we wasted wasn't the one you thought he was. The one you were looking for sold this camp to the dead guy."

"How in the fuck was I gonna know that? Let's get moving."

Then Kite went inside and got dressed and came back outside with a camera and took some pictures of the dead troopers and the man nailed up against the tree. They moved the two dead troopers under the tree where the other dead man was. The two killers smoked some crack and then began to walk away from the cabin. They first had removed the troopers weapons and badges and took them with them. Once they reached the atv they drove through the woods until they had traveled a good distance from the cabin where they had killed once again. They got into a small compact car that was parked on a dirt road hidden from sight. They then drove the short distant into New York State on a small dirt road that led into the near-by State Park, with camp grounds and cabins.

Captain Mason said to two troopers standing in front of him, "Go down to the area where Jones and Cutcher's GPS pointed them out to be and see why they haven't radioed for a pick-up by now. They should have completed their search by now."

Twenty minutes later a call came to Captain Mason from one of the troopers, "Captain, you better get down here and notify the crime scene techs and the ME. We have a big problem here!"

CHAPTER 4

Fear Surrounds Marshton

Portable lights were applied all around the new crime scene. Captain Mason said to the ME, "At least the killer didn't take the time to mutilate our troopers. It's going to be hell to notify the families.

I'm not looking forward to that."

"Better you than me. I don't envy you doing the notification. Jones and Cutcher were both family men, with little children."

"Do we know anything about the vic nailed to the tree?" Mason asked.

"I guess this was his cabin according to the info on the map. Also that is his truck out front. There were some photos in the glove compartment. He is from Jamestown, New York," the ME stated.

"This killer is one sick fucker. Placing the penis in the guy's mouth. I can't wait till we fry this bastard," Mason said.

"Our men were shot in their backs and in the head. What do you figure happened here captain?" The ME asked.

"Too early to tell for sure but they must have been taken by surprise to be hit in their backs. The head shots probably came after the fact," Mason related.

"I'm taking the bodies back now that the scene has been photographed. The techs will be quite awhile processing the scene. Talk to you later." The ME then left with the bodies.

Captain Mason walked to his car and placed a call to Norm Smithson. "Chief I have some bad news to report, there is another crime scene. Three more deaths and two of the dead are two of my troopers. It happened at a cabin owned by a man from Jamestown, New York; who was also killed and nailed to a tree with his dick stuffed in his mouth. I'm going to need your help as soon as possible. There's a crazy killer out here who seems to be killing just for the hell of it."

The police chief responded, "Just tell me what I can do to help and my force with do whatever we can."

"I have to get back to headquarters to call-in all shifts and notify families of the troopers' deaths. I'll call you from there with a plan of action. Right now I have troopers at some roadblock locations but we are short-handed until I can get other shifts involved."

The captain ended the call and the chief knew that the situation had escalated rapidly. He called in all shifts for duty and then placed a call to Mayor La Clare. The chief explained what Captain Mason just told him.

"We have to get the schools closed right now. I'll call Anne Jackson and she can use her authority to close the schools until further notice. She can then deal with the school board and Murphy. I'm sure she will do it once she hears what just happened in the woods," The mayor said.

"We are going to have to authorize a lot of overtime for our force until we catch the asshole."

"That's the least of our worries right now Norm."

"Well, we both have a lot to do now. Talk to you soon," the chief then ended his call.

Melissa Travers got a text message which read, "More lights in the woods. Another crime scene?"

"Penny, look at this text I just got."

Penny looked at the text and said, "We better put a hold on the article we wrote until we find out what is going on out there. I'm calling Chief Smithson to see if he will give us information."

After several busy signals the chief answered his phone. "Chief, this is Penny Sullivan and I will be right up front. Is there another crime scene in the woods? We have been told that there is one."

The chief thought a few seconds and then said, "Yes there is and I do not want to be quoted on this, but there are three more murders and two are state troopers. Now Penny, call Captain Mason for more information. I gave you more than I should but I live in this town and want our citizens protected."

"Thanks very much Norm. I really appreciate the truth." Penny ended her call.

"What did you find out?" Melissa asked her boss.

"There is another crime scene and three more murders. Two of which were state troopers."

"My god, no!" Melissa said in shock.

"We better get to work on a new front page article. I'll call state police headquarters while you get the layout ready." Sullivan called the state police headquarters but got the standard, "No comment at this time period."

"Did you get any more for the article?" Melissa asked.

"We go with what we have. We also have to warn our citizens. I need to call the mayor."

Mayor La Clare told Penny Sullivan that she was trying to get the schools closed as long as killer was roaming free out in the woods and that Anne Jackson was contacting the superintendent. The mayor said that she should hear back from Anne Jackson shortly and would call the newspaper so that the "schools closed" could be put in the paper.

Penny and Melissa began work on the front page for tomorrow's important edition of the paper.

The two killers drove to a camp that was rented at a State Park inside the New York State border. The Kite said, "Too bad you went nuts on Tom for throwing all that meth into the pond. He was such a good fuck."

"He wanted to quit and clean up his act. I think the fool was in love with his boyfriend that we have tied and gagged inside. Tom knew we were into this gig to get revenge on my brother Tat's death by these idiot's that live around here. Tom's boyfriend is going to do us some good real soon. So we keep him alive for now." The killer's brother had been killed by local residents in a massive shoot-out at a farm where Tat and two others had been staying. "We followed Tom and his boyfriend down that stream to where they dumped all of our meth we were going to sell. Tom chickened out on us. Throwing all that meth in that pond was the last straw. He got what he deserved."

"I'm coming down. Fire that pipe up again," Kite said as she hugged the man. Kite was in her late twenties and all the drugs she did hadn't had an affect on her very attractive body as of yet.

41

At The Marsh bar Jim Edwin and Jeff Bayern were talking about what made the coyotes attack golfers. The men came up with no apparent reason for the attack. Art Fisher, who was at a table with Jim Sparta said, "Maybe the coyotes just wanted to play-thru to the next hole."

Sparta added, "That is probably the stupidist thing that has come out of your mouth today."

Just then the phone rang and Cody Wayne answered and spoke into the phone for a few minutes. When he ended the call he said, "Rich Montana called to say that he saw troopers at another crime scene and that dead bodies were being loaded into a van. He was told to move along so he didn't know how many people were killed. He did see at least two body bags being carried to the van."

"Holy shit. What is going on in those woods? First the coyote attacks and then a dead body and now more dead bodies," Denny Wesfield said.

"Who is doing the killing?" Jill, the bartender asked.

"It would be nice if the state police would give the public some clues about who is doing the killing and why just in the area woods," Debbie Green added. The conversation continued in the bar, now focused on the recent killings just reported by Rich Montana.

Mayor La Clare called Penny Sullivan and related the information that it had been decided to close the schools for the rest of the week and hopefully that would be all that would be necessary. The residents were going to be warned to take precautions because a dangerous killer is out there and to take heed to protect yourself and your families The local radio will begin broadcasting the school district's concern immediately.

Penny Sullivan told the mayor that the school district's closing and a warning to Marshton's residents will be part of tomorrow's paper.

At the headquarters of the state police, Captain Mason had completed the difficult task of notifying the familes of the two troopers who were killed. He also contacted regional headquarters to relate to them about the two troopers who were murdered and asked for more assistance in terms of additional manpower to hunt down the killer. He was told by the regional headquarters that a special investigative unit would be arriving in the next day to coordinate the investigation with his troopers. In the meantime Mason called Chief Smithson and set up a meeting to use local police in the search to bring down the killer. The chief related to Mason that the district schools would be closed for the rest of the week. Mason agreed on that fact and also told the chief that "No Treaspassing" signs were being placed all along the wooded areas on North Road and that roadblocks had been set as he previously mentioned. He made it clear that no unauthorized persons should enter the woods. He also wanted the golf course to be closed, but the manager and golf pro, Al Conner didn't agree to that. Conner told the captain that the die hard golfers would be the only ones to play anyway after the animal attacks.

JK's Tavern was busy and the talk was about the road checks and about animal attacks and the killer at large. No one seemed to know any information on who was doing the killing or why. JK said to his bartender, Darcy Richards, "We had a problem like this awhile back where some nut cases were killing people in those woods. They even cooked and ate some."

Darcy looked shocked and said, "They even ate some people. What kind of insanity was that?"

"They got taken down in a fire fight by some regulars that come in here," Darcy's husband Bill said from the bar.

"So this is like a wild western tavern huh?" Darcy asked.

"Yeah, you can say that it is and I'm glad it is," JK said.

Penny Sullivan and Melissa Travers finished the front page story just in time to make it ready for press.

ALL MARSHTON SCHOOLS CLOSED!
THREE MORE MURDERS IN WOODS

Sullivan-Travers: Three more tragic murders have happened in the woods near North Road. The names of the deceased have not been released as of this printing but reports have been that two of dead are Pennsylvania State Police Troopers and one other victim. All signs point toward the same killer who is responsible for the recent deaths. As a result of the terror ongoing in the local woods, the Marshton District Schools will be closed for the scheduled school opening and for the rest of the week. Be advised that danger exists and all caution should taken by everyone.

Captain Mason, of the local state police detachment, had no comment at this time due to the deaths of his troopers and the terrible pain endured by families on hearing the news of the deaths of their loved ones. Our sympathy goes out to the familes and to fellow troopers. Please have patience at the roadblocks being used by the troopers in an attempt to locate the crazed killer.

(The front page article continued with comments from the school superintendent, the mayor and local chief of police.)

CHAPTER 5

Now A Fire

The next morning Alex and Sean were talking about the front page article in the Marshton paper. Sean said, "This is something that I never expected in your quiet little town. What is it now, four murders and coyote attacks on a golf course?"

"I'm as shocked as you are. I got a call earlier that the community college is closing for the rest of the week too. Hard to believe what is happening in those woods."

"If you want my opinion, I don't think it's done with. Closing the schools was a very smart move. I don't know about where you teach, but keeping kids away from the road where they could come into harm's way makes sense to me." Just then Sean's phone rang. It was his wife. "Hello honey. What's up with the early morning call?"

"I have good news. My parents booked us on a cruise. They paid for everything and said it was because of your brave actions in New York City. I think it's wonderful. Can you believe that?" Jesse said.

"That changes plans. That is quite a surprise to say the least. When are we scheduled to depart?" Sean asked.

"We depart from Miami in three days. Can you get a flight out in time?"

"I'm sure I can. I'll call right away and then let you know when I will get to the airport so you can meet me there. Tell your parents thanks for the great surprise."

"Ok, I think it will be great. Call me soon with the information. Love you so much and be careful up there because from what you told me earlier it doesn't sound too relaxing to me at Alex's."

"Love you too." Sean ended the call and said to Alex, "Well, well changes are afoot. Jesse's parents bought us passage on a cruise. So we can do the cruise and then fly into Buffalo and do the Fall's scene and then return here for a few days. How does that sound to you?"

"I think it will be great for you and Jesse," Alex said.

"I'll call to book a flight and that will be that. Now what were you asking me before Jesse called?"

"So you think the killer or killers aren't finished yet? Why?"

"We don't know what the motive behind the killings is. We don't have what was gathered at the crime scenes. We do know that torture was involved in the first killing, which represents some sort of rage involved. We know maybe drugs were involved to some degree and that the killings were basically done in the same general location. There was an old movie where two individuals go on a killing spree just for the hell of it. Killing for the sake of killing. I can't remember the name of it."

"Do you wish you could have all the information that the state police have?"

"It would give one a better starting point in the investigation, that's for certain. I just hope they have some good clues left at the crime scenes."

"What do you say we go out for breakfast? I know a great place called "Tracey's. All homemade cooking by a great cook," Alex said getting up from the kitchen table.

"Sounds like a plan."

Chief Smithson was meeting with his police force at the station. "I promised Captain Mason that we would be extra aware on our patrols and extend them out into the townships farther then we normally go. The state police are short-handed at this time and we need to give them our support."

Tom Rogers said, "All the killings have been in the same area and the troopers are covering that area so we don't go that far do we?"

"We can go out to Oak Road and back. Right near JK's Tavern and look for any shit going on in the woods on both sides of the road," the chief replied. "By the way overtime has been approved."

At the rented cabin in State Park the two killers were talking about their next moves. "So where and who do we hit next?" Kite asked.

"All those woods will be covered like glue by the troopers now that we axed two of their boys. I think we have to circle around and enter the town from where no one will expect us to."

"What in fuck do you plan to do in town? That's a bit too risky isn't it? It's risky too to keep Tom's boyfriend tied up with us."

47

"Don't worry about him. I'll think on it. Maybe you're right and we should lay low for a time. I could use a blow job while I'm thinking."

"So could I," Kite said and then began to unzip his pants.

The media ascended on Marshton after hearing about the terrible murders in the local woods. Reporters from Pittsburgh, Buffalo, Erie, Rochester and Philadelphia came into town along with several TV satellite trucks. Local motel and hotel rooms were filled with the out of town news people. The state police investigative team arrived and had to stay in a town twenty miles away from Marshton, due to lack of rooms in Marshton. Captain Mason directed media questions to the lead investigator, Isabelle Clarkson and her assistants, Jon Samuels and Jim Roberts. The only information given out by the state police was the names of those who had been killed in the woods. Other than that no other details were given to the media, who demanded more information.

Dr. Lee Stone, Jody Stone and Karen Hecate were having dinner at Abelli's and Mike Bombfield walked over to their table and said, "I heard that the two dead coyotes were tested for rabies and the test came back negative. So do I have to take the rest of those damn shots?"

Dr. Stone took a sip of his burbon and replied, "The test came back negative on those two coyotes, but there were more involved in the attack on the golf course."

Jody Stone added, "You better take those remaining shots just to be safe."

"What's the matter Mike, can't you stand the pain or don't you like our lollypops?" Karen said with a smile.

Mike looked at Karen and said, "I can take the pain ok but I'm not a fan of any shots."

Mike's girlfriend Joslynn said, "Be a big boy Mike and take the shots you need."

"I'll see you all when it's time for the next shot. Get some bigger suckers for my next shot." Mike then walked back to the bar with his arm around Joslynn.

Dr. Stone looked at his two nurses and said,"I'm glad he's going through with the whole series of shots for his sake."

It was midweek, after Labor Day, and at their camp the two killers were loading three five gallon cans of gas that they had bought in the nearby town of Jamestown, N.Y. It was three in the morning. "The roads should be pretty empty by now and we will park somewhere off the main road and walk to that fucking tavern where those assholes came from in that battle with my brother. It is so easy to avoid their roadblocks by using back roads. We're going to toast that place," Willy said.

"I got all of our shit packed up. Tom's boyfriend is tied on the floor of the car so he is no problem. So where are we going after we blow that place?" Kite asked.

"We have to stay a step ahead of the fuckers that are looking for us. So we go to a near-by town after we finish our job and hang out there for a few days. Then we decide what to do next and exactly how to use Tom's dear boyfriend."

The two left in the small car and drove near JK's Tavern and pulled off onto a small dirt trail, away from sight of the main road. They carried the gas cans through the woods and came in sight of the tavern.

They stopped suddenly, as a police car was turning around in the empty parking lot of the tavern. The car turned and headed back on the road to Marshton. The two killers then saw that it was clear to go down to the tavern. They placed a can of gas against the front door an opened the lid. They poured gas from another can all over the side wall and did the same in the back of the building. They walked into the woods and the Willy threw a lighted rag that had a stone wrapped inside against the building and the tavern burst into flames. They ran to their car and heard a very loud exploding noise as a can of gas blew up. They quickly left the scene and drove in the direction of Buffalo, New York using side roads.

It took the township volunteer fire department awhile to get assembled at the early morning hour and when the first truck arrived on the scene the tavern was engulped in a massive fire. The front of the building had broken inward and the rear of the building was about to fall down. Part of the roof had fallen down inside of the tavern. The fire was out within two hours and looked to be a total loss, according to Chip Cline, the fire chief.

JK, the owner of the tavern arrived at the fire scene and after the fire was out talked to Chief Cline about what he felt started the fire.

Chip Cline said, "It looks like it was arson to me. There are the remains of two gas cans, or what's left of gas cans. The fire inspector will determine the cause for sure when he gets here."

"Who in the hell would do this? I'd like to get my hands on the son-of-a-bitch," JK said in a most pissed off voice.

Chief Cline just shook his shoulders and stated, "At least no one was injured or killed. That was a hell of a fire and several tanks blew up inside that made things quite dangerous for us."

JK added, "I'm glad everybody's ok, but damn what a loss."

"I feel for you JK, but you have insurance don't you?" the chief asked.

"Yeah, I have enough to cover the loss but do I rebuild or not, that is the big question for me."

Police Chief Smithson was awakened by a call and told that JK's Tavern was on fire and he asked the officer calling if anyone was hurt?

The officer told him that he didn't know for sure, but a patrol car is on the way out there. The chief got dressed and had coffee and then left for the station to gather more information. When he arrived at the station he found out that the fire had been put out and that no one had been injured. He spoke on the radio to the patrol officer who was out on West Road. The officer told him that he had earlier turned around in JK's parking lot and everything was just fine at the time in the morning that he observed the tavern, The chief signed off after telling the officer to stay at the scene to see what he can find out. Norm Smithson went to get another cup of coffee and said out loud, "What next? Killings, animal attacks and now a damn fire."

CHAPTER 6

Still Question Marks

Media reports from Marshton were published in a great many newspapers and the internet was alive with chatter concerning the murders in the Marshton woods. The main details of the gruesome manipulation of two of the bodies had so far been kept out of the reporting by the media. Some residents of Marshton did know that bodies had been tortured because details had been in the Marshton Paper, but the majority of residents had no idea of the real violence that had taken place.

The state police continued to have no comment on the investigation and the special investigators had held no news updates thus far. Schools were due to reopen next week and there were no clues as to who was responsible for the murders in the woods. The woods had been totally searched and all cabins had also been searched. Not so much as a single fingerprint from any suspect had been discovered at any of the crime scenes. The state police thought that perhaps the killer had left the area; however, the roadblocks were to be continued for the rest of the week. Isabelle Clarkson, the lead investigator, said to Captain Mason, "The killer must have had on gloves, not to have left any prints at either crime scene. I would assume the first murder had been planned and the other crime scene murders took place when our troopers surprised the killer."

Mason replied, "I can't figure out how our men were shot in their backs. The killer must have ambushed them for that to happen."

Clarkson answered, "That could be true. It's not clear as of yet. You know we can't hold the media off for much longer. I'm going to have to give them something and soon."

"The problem is we don't have much to give them right now," Mason said.

"Did any more useful info come in on the first vic from Cleveland authorities?"

"Mason answered, "Nothing that will help us. Blackburn was a drifter and pretty much a loner."

"We need a break in this case. We are at a damn standstill."

"What about his family members?"

"They aren't any to be found anywhere," Mason again answered.

Isabelle Clarkson said, "Well I'm going to hold a news briefing after I contact the police chief and the mayor. I also need you to be there."

"Fine, I'll be there but we really don't have much to offer the press."

"I know but something is better than nothing. I'll hold the briefing at the local police station. I'll set it up for tomorrow after contacting the media. The FBI will be in town soon because of the killing of your troopers, so we need to be ready for them to appear on the scene."

The next afternoon the press briefing was held and several people gave what little information the investigation had to the press. Mayor La Clare announced when the public schools would reopen. The police chief stated that his force was working with the state police to help in the investigation. Lead investigator Clarkson stated that they were following several leads which she couldn't comment on in order to not compromise the investigation. Captain Mason announced the funeral dates for his two slain troopers and that additional troopers had been assigned to help with the investigation. FBI agent Steve Smith stated that he arrived to help with the investigation and wasn't yet briefed by Isabelle Clarkson, who ended the briefing by saying that in two days there would be another briefing at this location and the time would be announced. Reporters shouted questions at Clarkson, who turned and walked away with Captain Mason and the others.

Chief Smithson said to Mayor La Clare as they were walking away from the briefing, "Those reporters weren't happy with the information they got."

"I can't blame them. The investigation doesn't seem to have much to offer in terms of any progress," the mayor replied.

Alex Birch and Sean Burns were walking near the creek in front of Alex's house. "It's back to teaching for me next week. Must be the investigators think the killer is done or has left the area," Alex said.

"One can hope that he did, but hope doesn't work well where murder is concerned. People still need to be aware and careful."

"So you got your plane ticket set and you'll be off on the cruise to really do some relaxing?" Alex asked

"That's right. I am looking forward to the cruise and seeing Jesse. You know I've never been on a cruise before."

"I wish you a happy reunion and I'm looking forward to seeing Jesse when you return back here after the relaxing cruise and your trip to the falls. It has been quite awhile since I've seen Jesse."

"Yeah, it has and she is also looking forward to seeing you and the once peaceful town of Marshton."

"Do I detect sarcasm from the detective?"

Sean laughed and said, "Well murder has a way of turning what was once peaceful into a place just the opposite."

"Wise ass."

"Are you going to bring the woman you've been dating up to meet me or do I have to keep guessing what she looks like?"

"I will have her here when you and Jesse return from the falls. I told you that she teaches English and Creative Writing, with a concentration in poetry, at the college where I teach. Her name is Jeanene Belloc and she is smart and very attractive. I'm going to arrange a small cookout with some friends that want to meet the subway hero that was on all the national news stations, so you'll meet her then."

"Cut that hero shit out. I was just doing my job."

"Yes, but you stopped a massive bombing by doing that job."

"Yeah, yeah, basically, right place . . . right time and with a glock in my hand. Now how long have you been divorced my friend?"

"Divorce is really strange. At first you seem sorry that the marriage didn't work out. Then you feel a loss. Then you sense a rush of freedom that you didn't have for years. Then you just sort of get on another road of your life coping with everyday bullshit that comes along."

"Where are your children located these days?

"My son is at the University of Texas. He is in the athletic department. Coaches swimming and tennis. My daughter is in California and works for a large corporation that decorates movie stars homes."

"Sounds like you and your kids are doing just fine."

"How about your children?"

"Thomas works in publishing in Boston and Sarah lives in New York and is engaged to a guy who is into the Wall Street flow and she is going for her law degree." The men walked slowly back to Alex's house so Sean could pack for his flight.

At The Marsh bar, Carl Clapton, who owned his own computer business, was talking to Jeff Bayern, "So not much came out of that press briefing. Sounds like the investigators are clueless right now."

Jeff said, "They think we don't know about the sick torture or any other stuff that they are keeping from us."

Just then, Wanita Wallace and Bruce Bannon walked into the bar and Bannon said, "We just rode our bikes out to see JK's Tavern and it is burnt to the ground."

Wanita added, "We heard that someone torched the place on purpose."

Carl said, "With the murders and now arson, the cops have enough to keep them busy, that's for sure."

Tracy Springer, a contractor, asked, "I wonder if the roadblocks will be lifted soon, since the killer is probably long gone by now?"

"You would think that they would lift them because it would be stupid for the killer to hang around after killing two troopers. The state police have to be plenty pissed about two of their own being killed," Bannon stated.

Wanita said, "JK is no doubt just as pissed about his place being burnt down as the state police are about two of their own being killed."

At the Marshton Golf Course, Al Conner was looking at the back of pro shop door that had been smashed inward. The garbage cans near the door were spread about and the garbage was dumped out of all of the cans. There were bear tracks all around. Conner said to one of the men who worked on the grounds, "Looks like a bear tried to smash its way into the club and then did a number on the garbage cans. I'm calling the game warden. He walked inside and got Ben Wooley on the phone. He explained what had happened and Wooley told him that he would be there soon to see the situation.

In a room of a cheap motel in Buffalo, Willy was on top of the Kite, who was moaning as the man pushed in and out of her. She dug her fingers into his back as she reached orgasm. She looked up at him and said, "That coke makes fucking all the better."

Willy said, "Rubbing it on your pussy helps baby." They got up and both did another line of coke. "We are going back to that fucking town and do some more damage. Are you up for it?"

"Whatever you want. Got any plans in mind?"

The man answered, "Yeah I do and this time some of those fuckers who killed my brother are going to pay for it. Plus it's time to use Tom's boyfriend to our advantage."

"How you going to use him?"

"He's going to be responsible for the killings. You'll soon see."

"We burnt down that bar. What else can we do to get any of them?"

"There's a lot we can do and we will do it."

"Ok babe, now how about kissing my pussy for a time. I'm still horny."

"Sounds like your clit will be my cocaine popsickle."

CHAPTER 7

A Calm Comes To The Town

Jim Roberts, the assistant investigator from state police headquarters was talking with Captain Mason, "Isabelle and Jon left for our regional headquarters on orders. We cancelled the upcoming news briefing due to the fact Carson Thomas, our boss at headquarters, believes that the killer has fled the local area and he feels that the search for the killer has to expand state and perhaps nationwide."

"Maybe it makes sense that the killer has left the area? We have stopped all roadblocks at this point in time and honestly, there simply aren't any clues out there to make us think the killer is still around. But I'm not so sure about that. So when are you leaving?" Mason asked.

"Carson Thomas wants me to stay for another three or four days to wrap things up here."

"You mean just in case we are wrong and the damn killer reappears, which I most certainly hope doesn't happen. Things are getting back to normal with schools all open again and no roadblocks and we have removed the no trespassing signs."

Mason thought to himself "what an ass this Roberts was and probably this Thomas guy was too."

Melissa Travers reached the golf course and approached two men who were talking in front of the pro shop. She walked over to the men and introduced herself. She then asked, "Anything new on the animal attacks as of late?"

Both men looked at each other with surprised glances. Al Conner said, "As a matter of fact come with me out back." The three of them walked to the rear of the pro shop. "This just happened."

Melissa looked at the caved-in door and the crushed garbage cans. "What happened back here? Did some animal do this? She then took her camera out and snapped some pictures of the scene.

Ben Wooly said, "It was a bear that did this, that's for sure. Looks like he tried to smash his way through the door."

Al Conner added, "The door bent inward but the bear didn't get inside. I've had garbage dumped before but that's why there are heavy steel lids on the cans and the dumpster is always kept shut. There's never been a bear that actually tried to break inside before. That's a first."

Wooly added, "You know Ron Macintine told me that a big bear charged into his jeep recently and tried to get in his jeep. It happened on North Road."

"You mean he was driving his jeep when the bear attacked? When did that happen?" Melissa asked in amazement in her voice.

"Right around the time of those crazy coyote attacks on the course," Wooly replied.

Melissa was busy taking down notes and then said, "Well thank you for the information. She then took a photo of the two men in front of the caved-in door. She then left the golf course. In her mind she wanted to talk with Ron Macintine as soon as she could locate him in order to get more details on the bear attack on him and his jeep.

After his class, Alex walked across the campus to Dr. Belloc's classroom. She was talking with a student and glanced at Alex with a smile. The student said, "Thank you for the help Dr. Belloc," and then left.

"Hello Jeanene, or should I say, Dr. Belloc?" Alex said as he smiled at her.

"Very funny Alex. So are you ready for a nice glass of wine and perhaps a meal?"

"I definately am."

"By the way Alex, when am I going to meet the hero friend of your's from New York City?"

"When he returns from the cruise he is going on with his wife. I am having a get together at my house. They are going to fly into Buffalo after the cruise to see the falls and then they will be returning here for a stay. So my dear you will meet Jesse and Sean then."

As they walked to one of the campus parking lots Jeanene said, "I am looking forward to the meeting. What can I offer to bring to your little party?"

"Just bring you beautiful personality and charm."

Penny Sullivan was meeting with Mayor La Clare in the mayor's office. Penny asked, "So what you are telling me is that the special investigators left town and all roadblocks have been taken down.

Schools are back to normal. So we are to pretend the whole damn thing didn't happen? Whose great idea was that?"

The mayor answered, "Captain Mason informed me that the lead investigator, Isabelle Clarkson, got orders to leave by her boss, who feels that the killer has left our area and to remain here without any additional clues to the killings would simply be a waste of resources and money. Also the extra troopers will be going back to their normal stations."

"So the murders remain unsolved and the investigation is over?"

Mayor La Clare answered, "It's not over but has been moved to the regional headquarters. They aren't going to stop the investigation until the killer has been caught. I hope they are right about the killer having left our location."

"That makes two of us. I feel so sorry for the trooper's families and that poor man from Jamestown who was just in the wrong place."

"Yes, the murders are tragic to say the least."

The meeting ended and Sullivan went back to her office and thought about tomorrow's front page while her other reporters worked on their assignments.

CHAPTER 8

An Explosive Fury

Ken "Mouse" James drove his truck into the parking lot of the Volunteer Fire Department where bingo was soon to let out. He came to pick up his wife Becky. Mouse got out of his truck and walked to the door of the fire hall and waited for the last game to end. In the dim lighted parking lot a dark figure crawled under the truck which Mouse had just parked. The figure sliced a rubber connector on the gas line and quickly crawled out from under the truck. Mouse was walking to his truck with his wife. They were twenty yards away. The dark figure shot a small wooden arrow that was aflame under the truck from where he crouched behind another truck. Suddenly, Mouse's truck exploded and Mouse was knocked to the dirt parking lot along with his wife. Two other cars also caught fire. People were running away from the burning flames. The dark figure was no where to be seen.

An hour later all the flames had been estinguished and the burnt truck and cars were simply burnt remains. Mouse had a cut on his head and his wife asked him, "Are you sure you're ok?"

Mouse replied, "I think I know how a NFL player feels on concussion protocol now. My head hit the parking lot. He looked at his truck and shook his head.

Becky said, "What caused all that to happen?"

"I don't know but I'm glad we weren't inside or we wouldn't be talking right now."

"We can always replace the truck but not each other." Becky then kissed her husband lightly on the cheek.

Janet Montana walked over to Becky and Mouse and said, "I finally win a bingo jackpot and I walk out and my car was on fire. How's that for luck?"

Becky answered, "You are lucky because you could have been in the car."

Chip Cline, Volunteer Fire Department Chief walked over to Mouse and asked, "Too bad about your truck. It's a total waste."

Mouse looked at the remains of his truck and said, "It's only a year old. I liked that truck too."

"Did you have a gas leak in a line or the engine? The reason I'm asking because the fire seemed to begin in your truck first."

"No I didn't have any leak that I was aware of. The truck ran great and I just had a check-up a month ago and nothing was wrong with it"

"Well what could have started the fire? People saw the explosion burst from your truck and it had to be from something that touched off the gasoline."

"Chip, I have no idea what caused it. I just don't know what to tell you."

"The fire inspector won't be able to tell much even if there was a gas leak because of what's left of the truck. Hell, most of the key lines are melted or fused together. It's a shame."

Far away now from the truck explosion the dark figure laughed at the woman driving the car and said, "That worked perfect. Who would think that a kid's cheap bow and arrow set could do that. I mean after I crawled under the truck without anyone seeing me and cut that rubber connection to the gas line and then let some gas drain and then shot a flaming arrow wrapped with a rag soaked with a little gas under that truck . . . . then boom!"

"You did what you started out to do. Now where are we going to stay tonight?" Kite asked.

"Yes, but I wanted to fry those assholes but I didn't have time to.

Drive to that town called Salamanca. It's close by. It will be a busy day tomorrow and I need to take a walk into a rocky area some miles from here."

"Why do you have to do that?"

"I need to catch something. That's why I have the long stick in the back."

"I'm not going with you. I'll stay at the motel with our captive friend in the backseat, still nice and tied."

"Ok, but don't smoke any shit while I'm gone. Just do some coke, you can't smell that. Soon we'll be rid of Tom's boyfriend."

"Can I at least fuck him in the ass? He might like that."

"Leave him tied and don't fuck with him."

The Marshton Paper ran a story on the fire at the fire hall after bingo was letting out. There was no cause of the fire in the story other then a suspected gas leak in a truck as the possible cause. No clear reason was given as how the gas leak burst into flames, if indeed it was a gas leak. However, Fire Chief Cline tended to point toward a gas leak as the cause when he was interviewed. He stated when questioned that due to the nature of the truck explosion that gasoline had to have been involved. He felt very lucky that there were no serious injuries. He also laughed when he said that at least we didn't have far to go to put out the fires. The paper showed a photo of the aftermat of the fire on the front page.

There was also a story in the paper of the bear who tried to smash his way into the golf pro shop and also the bear who attacked Ron Macintine's jeep. Photos were included in the story of both the pro shop door and Macintine's jeep. Game Warden Wooly stated in the article that bears do unexpected things at times and that is why people need to be very careful around any bear.

Later that night Willy crept near a truck parked in a driveway that was owned by Mike and Patty Mayer. He was going to insert a thin metal rod in the window area of the truck to force the window down several inches but the door was unlocked. He then forced something into the truck out of a thick bag. He then pushed on the door until it was closed. He then left the scene without any one seeing what he had done. Then he walked into the nearby woods and then down a path and finally got into a car with Kite behind the wheel. The car quickly left the scene.

The next morning Mike and Patty Mayer walked to their truck and both started to enter the truck. Suddenly, Mike yelled as a rattlesnake sprung at him and bit him on the arm. "Watch out Patty! I got bit by a snake!"

Patty ran around the truck to where her husband was holding his arm. She saw a snake crawling away through the grass. She immediately helped her husband into the truck and drove off toward the hospital. In the truck Mike said, "It was a rattlesnake. How did it get inside the truck?"

Patty said, "I don't know but stay still so the poison won't spread. We'll be at the hospital soon." Luckily, they only lived a few miles from the hospital. When they arrived at the emergency room Mike was taken directly in to be treated. Dr. Danielle Steelman looked at Mike's arm and said, "How in the world did you get bitten by a rattlesnake? The fangs are still in your arm."

"The damn thing was in my truck."

The doctor removed the fangs and gave Mike an anti-venom injection. "You are lucky you live so near. That venom can spread quickly. I'd like you to stay for a day just to make certain you don't have any reactions to the injection, which some people do. Not that we get that many people who have been bitten."

Patty walked back to where Mike had been treated and said,"The doctor told me that you'll be staying the night as a precaution. She kissed Mike and said,"Mike that was so scary. Where do you think it came from?"

"I don't Patty, but at least it got my arm and not my pretty face."

"This is no time for jokes dear."

Hospital staff came to take Mike to a room and he said to his wife,

"I'll see you in the room. Are you going to work today?"

"I am certainly not. I'm going to be with you. Besides, I'm too nervous to do any work. I'll see you in your room."

In the motel room, in Salamanca, "How in the fuck did you learn to catch a damn rattlesnake?" the amazed Kite asked.

"You can learn anything online. It was no big deal. I just hope that snake bit those two fuckers who were involved in killing my brother."

"Are we about done with this revenge adventure of your's? We should get away from here while the gettin's good."

"We will soon but there's some more to do first. Now we need to change motels. Lucky we still have lots of cash left from those three break-ins in Ohio."

"What's more important is we have lots of drugs left to get us by."

The man laughed and they both did a line of coke.

Penny Sullivan was talking with Melissa Travers in the editor's office. "You know I called Captain Mason again and he related to me that there was no new information to be had on the investigation. He did say that the investigation is still active and will be active until the killer is caught. He did say that a $50,000 dollar reward has been offered for the capture and conviction of the killer. He gave me a tip line phone number, which we can print in our next issue. Actually, he was quite nice on the phone for the first time.

"Well, he is still under a lot of pressure to come up with some clues as to who murdered those four victims and why they were murdered."

"We can guess why the troopers were killed Melissa. They probably were ambushed by the killer at the cabin where the victim who owned the cabin was killed. We have no clue as to why the first victim was killed and tortured and neither do the state police as far as we know."

"Also we have those animals near the golf course going crazy and the one bear attacking that jeep on North Road. We still have no answers as to why all that happened. Not even the hunters I spoke to can understand any of it."

"I know what you mean. It seems we are at a brick wall to say the least. Maybe that FBI guy can help solve the case."

CHAPTER 9

Terror At An End?

At the very small motel outside of Marshton, a man checked into a room using the identification of Tom's boyfriend. It was dark outside and it was easy for the man and woman to bring the man they were holding hostage into their room, as no cameras were near where their room was located and the man behind the check-in counter was busy watching a baseball game. Once inside the room, the man was put on the bed and was unconscious. Willy picked up a trooper's pistol that had been taken from one of the dead troopers. He pointed it in a plastic bottle and put the end of the bottle into the unconscious man's mouth and with his gloved hand he put the unconscious man's hand on the gun's trigger so it would look like a self-inflicted wound as Willy pulled on the trigger and blew the man's head apart. The shot was silenced so no one could hear, as the TV was also turned up loud. Next, bloody clothing from the first and second victims was tossed in a pile in a corner of the room and one of the dead trooper's badges was put into the now dead man's pocket. The scaling knife was also laid on the floor under the bed. Then a note was placed on the bed which said, "I loved Tom and I'm sorry that I killed all of them. The meth made me go crazy." Lastly, some meth was sprinkled on the bed and on the man's body. Kite and Willy made sure nothing could tie them to the room.

When the man and woman killers walked outside the room and shut the door, Willy said in a low voice, "We have Tom's boyfriend's prints on the steering wheel and on the dash and glovebox. Tom's ID is in the glovebox and two weapon's of the troopers are in the trunk, with prints on the weapons we placed there.

"You got it baby. Let's get the fuck outta here," Kite said as she smiled. They got into another stolen car that was parked nearby.

The next day, Alex ran out of his house as he saw a car pull into his driveway. He knew it was Sean and Jesse returning from the falls. He greeted them with a huge smile. "Nice tans, you two," and he hugged Jesse and Sean.

"Well let me help you with your luggage and a cold beer awaits you on the patio and there is wine if you'd prefer Jesse," Alex said.

Once Sean and Jesse got seated on the patio they told Alex about their cruise and the stops the ship made along the way and how great the Mayan ruins were to walk about in and how the falls were so good to finally see, Sean added, "We remembered not to drink the water or use ice in our drinks while in Mexico, so we didn't get Montezuma's Revenge, like you did on your trip to Mexico."

Alex laughed and replied, "Yes I remember being on the toilet for some time after using ice in my drinks. Stupid mistake on my part."

Jesse said, "This is such a nice view you have here, with the pine trees surrounding your land and the huge yard. Do you get many animals wondering through the yard?"

"Yes, lots of deer, mainly, but foxes, squirrels and sometimes a bear or two."

Sean smiled when he said, "But no attacking coyotes I hope."

Jesse looked at Alex with a worried look and Alex shook his head and answered, "No, no coyotes that I have ever seen."

Jesse looked at ease and asked, "So are things resolved in your town with the murders and animal attacks?"

"Things seem back to normal, but nothing has really been solved in either case as far as I know. All schools are up and running as is the college. Oh Sean, I hope you won't mind too much but the local paper's editor called and asked me if she could do a story on you when you returned. She must have found out that you were in town and you being so famous as you are, she wants to stop up and talk with you."

"That would be so nice dear," Jesse said smiling.

"Damn you Alex. You probably set this all up."

"No I didn't. She could have heard about you being here from Carla at Abelli's."

"So when is this going to take place?" Jesse asked.

"I told her I'd let her know today. Come on it will be fun Sean," Alex said.

Sean took a big sip of his beer and stated, "Fine give her a call and let's get it over with."

Jesse leaned over and kissed Sean.

"I'll call her now," Alex said as he picked up his phone.

When Alex put down his phone he looked at Sean and said, "She was very excited to be able to talk to a real hero. She'll be here directly."

"Wonderful," Sean said with no glee in his voice.

Penny Sullivan arrived within thirty minutes with her photographer and also Melissa Travers, her main reporter. After introductions, the interview started with Penny Sullivan, Melissa Travers, Sean and Jesse at one patio table and Alex moved to another table to listen to the happenings. After forty-five minutes and several photos later it was over, thanks to Sean's relief.

When the Marshton Paper's staff left, Sean immediately said, "I need a beer and no more of this bullshit while I'm here Mr. Alex Birch."

"You did good Sean from what I heard," Alex said to his friend.

"You were great sweetie. That must have been hard to relive that entire scene for you," Jesse said.

"Yeah, well it happened and it's over and done with and so is this beer. One more please, my press agent."

Alex laughed and got Sean another beer and Jesse was ready for one also.

At a motel on the outskirts of Marshton, a maid knocked on the door of a room she was to clean. There was no answer from anyone inside so she used a pass key to open the door. What she saw made her quickly turn away and run to the motel's small office. The manager returned to the room with her and was shocked to see a dead man on the bed with his head blown apart. The manager and the maid quickly returned to the office and the manager called the Marshton police.

A year ago there would have been township police to call, but due to budget cuts the Marshton town police would be the quickest response. The state police would take longer to arrive. When Chief Smithson took the call from the motel manager he processed what the manager was telling him about a blood bath in one of his rooms. The chief tried to calm down the manager and told him not to enter the room and that both the Marshton police and the state police would be there directly.

Chief Smithson ended the call and then called Mark Mason of the state police and gave him the directions to the motel and said that he would meet him at the location. He also told Captain Mason to bring a medical examiner and a crime scene unit because of the bloody scene that the manager had described to him.

Jim Roberts was scheduled to leave today, however, Captain Mason told him he might want to delay his departure until the newest crime scene was viewed to make sure it was not related to the murders in the woods. Roberts agree and said that he would go with Mason to the recent crime scene.

When Chief Smithson arrived at the motel with officer Tom Rogers, they both looked into the bloody room and did not enter in order not to corrupt the crime scene. Rogers said, "Looks like the guy on the bed killed himself. The gun is still in his hand."

"There's blood sprayed on the wall behind the bed, so yeah it does seem that he did himself in that's for sure," the chief said while still looking into the room through the open door.

Captain Mason soon arrived with the troopers to process the scene.

Mason walked into the room followed by his ME and crime scene techs.

The ME handed Captain Mason the note that was on the bed. Mason read the note and then walked over to Chief Smithson and let him read the note without touching it.

Smithson looked at Mason and said,"Looks like that note gives us a lot of answers to the murders."

Mason held the note in his gloved hands and replied,"It appears that it does and that glock in the dead man's hands is from one of my dead troopers, so it came from the scene where my troopers were killed."

Jim Roberts from the regional headquarters looked at the note Mason held and stated,"Well that as they say is that. Looks like I can call headquarters and report what transpired here."

One crime scene tech called Mason over to a corner in the room to look at a pile of bloody clothing and then another tech found a scaling knife from under the bed and showed the captain. A photographer was also busy snapping photos of the entire scene as the crime scene techs continued to work. Meanwhile outside the car parked in front of the room was being searched after the keys had been taken from the dead man's pants, where a trooper's badge had also been found in the man's pocket. When the trunk of the car was opened trooper's weapons were found. FBI agent Steve Smith checked the crime scene out and read the note Mason held, but didn't comment. He did jot down notes.

Captain Mason walked over to Chief Smithson and said, "There's really nothing you can do here anymore. We have a lot of processing to do and I want to thank you for your quick response to the scene."

The chief looked at Mason and said, "Well I don't envy you and your team, but at least you can bring a close to the fear that has been haunting this community."

"I certainly hope I can bring some closure to my dead troopers' families and to this community. Thanks again."

Mason then walked back into the bloody room and Chief Smithson and his officer walked over to their car.

Jim Roberts was on his phone talking with Carson Thomas at regional headquarters. He gave him all the details found so far at the motel room, which pointed in the direction that the man who killed the troopers and others in the woods was now dead himself. The manager identified the dead man as the one who registered in the motel. Thomas told Roberts to remain in Marshton for another day while processing continued. He ended the call by saying, "Looks like this case has come to an end without additional, innocent deaths. See you soon. I'll make a statement to the press, who have been on my ass. It will give me great pleasure to get those bastards off my back at last."

CHAPTER 10

What Next?

A lex drove Sean and Jesse on a scenic drive to a favorite local restaurant called The Y Bar, which was located a few miles from Marshton. Alex knew the owner and his wife Debbie. When they walked inside Alex waved to Bill, the owner and said, "I brought my friends here for some of your famous lunch choices."

Bill came over to Alex and shook hands and was introduced to Jesse and Sean. They sat at a table and Bill brought over menus and took drink orders. Jack, the bartender waved at Alex. Jack was also one of the best pool shots in the area and seldom lost a game.

Alex and Sean ordered one of the special cheeseburgers that the bar was known for and Jesse ordered a salmon salad. All three had beer to drink. When their lunch was over Bill came over to the table and talked with Alex and his friends about what was happening at his bar and that they should stop over at night for dinner sometime. Before they left the bar Bill gave Sean and Jesse both Y Bar tee shirts. They waved so long to Jack and Bill.

"That was one cool bar and the owner and bartender were also very nice people," Sean said and Jesse agreed.

Penny Sullivan had just completed her article about the hero detective and asked Melissa Travers to read over it before it went to print.

A Hero Visits Marshton

Sullivan: Sean Burns, the New York City hero, homicide detective who prevented a terrorist bombing in the subway system recently, is in Marshton to visit his friend Alex Birch and recover from a gunshot wound he received as he put his life in real danger to stop the bombers from blowing up the subway station and causing many thousands of deaths.

Sean talked with this paper's editor and reporter, Melissa Travers and related how his actions were needed and deadly, did prevent the terrorists from their mission in killing those innocent New Yorkers who were subway passengers.

Sean was decorated for his actions by the governor of New York and also by the mayor of the city. He also has been invited to the White House by the president. It is indeed a special honor to have Sean and his wife, Jessica, in Marshton. May your wound heal quickly and thank you for all that you have done.

There were photos of Sean, Jesse and Alex around the article on the front page.

FBI agent Steve Smith went inside the local police station and asked to speak with Chief Smithson. The chief stood up from his desk and shook the agent's hand. "Have a seat. What can I do for you?"

Smith sat down and said, "Well chief I'm leaving today since the case has been closed by the state police."

"Yes, head of the regional headquarters of the state police made that choice and there's nothing that can be done about his closing the case," the chief stated. Agent Smith shook hands with the chief and left the office.

Soon after the FBI agent left the chief's office the phone on his desk rang. The chief picked up the phone and it was Captain Mason, who said, "Chief I know the case has been closed by the head of regional headquarters and what I am going to say to you has to stay between you and me. Is that clear to you? Do I have your trust?"

The chief felt sort of strange by what Mason related, but said, "Sure."

"I have some doubts about closing the case. I mean that entire motel scene seems somewhat too pat. That motel manager for example really didn't pay much attention to the man when he signed into the motel. He said he was watching a damn baseball game when the guy signed in. Then the room itself was loaded with clues. Maybe I'm way off, but then perhaps I'm not."

"But the trooper's gun was in the man's hand and the weapons found in the car's trunk belonged to the troopers," the chief replied.

"I know what you are saying. It all seems to fit. I'm trying to get more information on the dead vic in the motel room. His DNA is all over the room, that's for certain and his prints were on the knife and on the troopers' weapons. It looks like an open and shut case but maybe, just maybe, it is supposed to look that way."

"What do you plan to do about it? I mean, how can I help you?"

"The state police can't help any more because the case is closed as far as they are concerned. I'm not sure what I'm going to do yet. I've learned to trust my feelings and this just doesn't feel right to me."

"Well if you decide you need my help, just let me know."

"Thanks chief and remember to keep this between us. No one can know that I plan to keep looking into the case, even if Carson Thomas feels the case is closed. I owe it to my two dead troopers."

"You can trust me captain and I will do all I can to help you."

"Thanks again chief and I'll be in touch soon."

CHAPTER 11

A Party And More

It was a clear evening and Alex and Sean had built a bright burning fire in the large fire pit. There were chairs situated around the fire pit and Alex had placed food on a table on his patio. The food consisted of wings, pizza, and lots of snacks. Jeanene Belloc had been introduced to Jesse and Sean earlier in the day when Alex brought her to his house.

There were several other people who had arrived for the party and now the talk around the fire pit had centered on the latest school shooting. Jesse said, "In most of the school shootings automatic weapons have been used and still Congress has done nothing to eliminate these weapons out of the hands of the killers."

Jeanene stated, "They keep lowering the government flags and saying prayers for the dead, but still they do nothing about stricter background checks and those deadly weapons."

"Right and all the time children of all ages continue to die in all kinds of schools," said Scott Travis, one of Alex's neighbors.

"It seems like we are going to have to make our schools into damn forts," Alex stated.

"At least the schools need armed guards or maybe some teachers who have weapons," Sandy Larsen said. Sandy was a teacher in the Drama Department at the community college.

Alex asked, "What do you think about it Sean?"

"If our children were still in school, I'd want them protected as best as possible and if that meant arming some teachers or guards, I'd be for it, but that might not stop the attacks in itself. Look at the recent attack. A fire alarm was pulled and children were shot. Killers normally plan the attack and somehow gain entrance into buildings, even with guards in the buildings," Sean replied.

"So what is the answer?" Jesse asked.

Alex said, "We spend billions upon billions of dollars on foreign aid and on our current wars and in countries like Syria and we short change our educational systems. We should protect our own children first before involvement in other nations. Make tighter laws before some nut can buy a weapon like an AR-15."

Jeanene mentioned, "First, we need a government that will care enough to do something. Right now all we get is talk, talk, and more talk. Meanwhile, our children become more and more targets in our schools."

Scott said, "We need to vote out the members of congress that will do nothing and see who is funding these do-nothings and bring attention to them."

Jesse added, "Money talks in our government. It always has. If people would start voting out those in Congress who are tied into the money from organizations like the NRA, perhaps we would get people in office who would actually do something positive."

"Dylan said a great line, "Money doesn't talk . . . it swears," and truer words were never spoken," Alex stated.

Another neighbor of Alex's named Jackson said, "You know the NRA does a lot of good, like gun safety courses and hunter safety classes. There are millions of automatic weapons in this country now. If someone wants to get their hands on one they probably can."

As the night wore on the conversation switched to our nation's drug problems and then to college and pro sports.

Captain Mason did know before the case had been closed by regional director Thomas, that the dead man in the motel room had been arrested in Ohio for male prostitution on two occurrences. That seemed to tie into the note that had been left in the room. He also learned that the motel manager and the maid claimed the $50,000 reward offered in the case and that could be why they wanted the man in the room to be the one responsible for the killings. Mason said to himself, "It could make sense that he was the killer, but damn, I just don't know. Damn!"

The two killers left their motel room in a town close to Marshton and drove into the town Marshton. "What are we going to do if the guy isn't home?" the Kite asked.

"We wait until the fucker comes home and then he'll get what's coming to him. And if we leave no prints, nothing will lead back to us. That's why we wear gloves like we did in the woods. Got it?"

Kite shook her head to signal yes. Willy drove the car to a location just outside of Marshton. It was near midnight and the man drove his car past two other houses on the road and parked his car where the paved road turned to dirt and there were no other houses in sight. Then Willy and Kite got out of the car and walked toward the house they were looking for. The two other houses were at least fifty yards from the house where they hoped their next victim would be.

They could see a light on in the house and they smiled at each other.

They walked quietly up to a window and the Willy peeked in the window and saw the man they were hoping to find, passed out in a chair in front of a TV set that was still on.

Willy spoke in a whisper to the woman, "Give me the needle."

Kite answered, "It's all loaded to put the asshole into a permanent sleep."

Willy walked onto the porch and tried the door. He smiled as the door opened. Kite followed the Willy inside and held a pistol in her hand in case their potential victim woke up. Kite watched as Willy injected the man in the chair with a lethal dose of heroin. The man in the chair opened his eyes as the needle penetrated his arm but fell back into the chair and his head fell to one side. He was dead! Kite then put a small container of heroin on the floor beside the chair and then placed the syringe into the dead man's hand. She smiled and the two killers left the house and walked to their car. They turned the car around and left the headlights off as they did when they drove up to their destination. They left the car's headlights off until they were several hundred yards from the now dead man's house. Kite said, "That went well. That guy never knew what happened to him."

"And he never will wake up to find out." They both laughed. They then drove to a motel back in the town of Salamanca.

The party was over at Alex's house and Sean, Jesse, Jeanene and Alex were still around the fire pit. Alex asked, "So when are you two New Yorkers planning to head back to the big city?"

Sean looked at Jesse and then said," I guess in a few more days, if you don't mind putting up with us."

"You are welcome to stay as long as you so desire. It's great having you here," Alex replied.

Jeanene then said, "Jesse and I are going to go shopping in Erie tomorrow. I told her about all the malls there and the outlet stores.

That will give you both a chance to watch football together."

"That sounds good to me. How about you Sean?" Alex asked.

"Right, I can get up for some football and beer," Sean said.

"Just make sure you walk to town and not drive. Your leg seems much better so it will do you good to walk," Jesse said.

"Can I at least stagger on the way back from town," Sean said with a smile on his face.

Jesse lightly punched Sean's arm and said, "Try not to over do it."

"Well, if we are going to have a big day of football and beer tomorrow, I for one need to get some rest and my beautiful wife promised to massage my leg," Sean said.

Jeanene looked at Alex and smiled at Sean's comment. Alex put the fire out in the pit and walked with Jeanene into the house. Sean and Jesse walked into the guest room and closed the door. Alex and Jeanene had a cup of coffee and then went into Alex's bedroom.

CHAPTER 12

A Sunday Happening

Jesse and Jeanene had left for their trip to Erie in order to shop in the many stores and malls. Sean and Alex were seated around a table on Alex's patio. Both men were having their second cup of coffee. It was 10:30 in the morning and the weather was clear and sunny. Alex looked over at Sean and asked, "So who do you like in today's game?"

"Well I know that you are a Bills fan and since they are playing the Steelers today, I am going with the Steelers. As you know I am a Giants fan and have been for as long as I can remember. Your team has improved as of late but not enough to beat the Steelers."

"Your Giants are playing the Patriots and that means big trouble for your team."

"True but as the saying goes, *On any given Sunday . . .*"

"Well we shall see what we shall see. Now how about we start getting ready to walk into town. I usually watch the first half of the game at Abelli's and the second half at The Marsh."

"Sounds good to me," Sean said as he got up from the table.

At The Marsh bar, people were talking about the death of Robert Browning, while waiting for the Steelers—Bills game to start. Jeff Bayern said, "It was a real shocker that Browning died of an overdose.

I never thought he was into any kind of drugs."

Art Fisher added, "He just went through a divorce and was laid-off from work, so maybe he got involved in drugs. Who the hell knows what drove him to drugs?"

Jim Sparta said, "It's too bad to see any one get hooked on hard drugs. If a person is going to get addicted to something make it alcohol or even pot."

"Right, that way you can have a smile on your face and eat munchies," Fisher replied.

"The cops ruled it an overdose and he knew he could die from using that shit and he did die. I feel sorry for him, but he did it to himself," Cody Wayne stated.

"I agree with what Cody said and now give us all a drink so we can feed our addiction . . . beer," Hoss said.

Judy, the bartender, smiled and said, "At least this addiction is legal." She then began to put beers on the bar.

Just when Sean and Alex were ready to leave for their walk into town, Alex's phone rang. Alex answered, "Hello Chief, how goes it?"

The call was from Chief Smithson, who asked Alex if Sean was still in town. Alex said that he was still here and that they were ready to walk into town to watch some football. The Chief asked Alex to put Sean on the phone.

Sean looked shocked as Alex handed Sean his phone and said, "The local chief of police would like to talk to you."

Sean took the phone and said, "This is Sean, what can I do for you?"

DAVID CLOSE

"I would like to talk with you about the recent murders that happened in our woods."

Sean still semi-shocked said, "I thought they found the guy responsible for those killings. He was found dead in a motel room wasn't he?"

"Well it appeared that he was responsible but both myself and the state police captain aren't quite sure about the facts in the case, even if Carson Thomas, the regional commander closed the case. You would do us a big favor if we could meet with you to talk about the case. I know you are visiting Alex and we can meet with you Tuesday at a time you can name."

"Well this is a surprise to me. But if you think I can help I'll meet with you at Alex's at say noon on Tuesday."

"That would be great. Thanks we'll see you then. You and Alex enjoy the game today and thanks again."

Sean ended the call and looked at Alex. "Your chief wants to meet with me Tuesday, along with the state police captain to discuss the murders that happened in your woods. They don't agree with the facts at hand that led to the closing of the case. What in hell is this all about?"

"I have no idea. So you are going to meet with them?"

"I said I would. We are meeting here at noon Tuesday."

"That could prove interesting indeed."

"Well, yeah it could be interesting that they don't agree that the case was closed just simply to close the case before the real killer or killers are caught. There's something in the wind here and what it is isn't clear. Perhaps we will find out Tuesday. Now let's do some football and beer."

Alex pulled on his Buffalo Bills shirt and said, "Ok, off to see the Bills thump the Steelers!"

Sean smiled and said, "Any thumping to be done and it will be by the Steelers." They then left Alex's and began their walk into town.

At Abelli's, Dr. Lee Stone, Jody Stone, Dr. Ron Brown and his wife were having lunch after a round of golf played at the local golf course. "That was certainly a strange happening. To see all those crows flying at the clubhouse," Dr. Stone said.

Jody added, "It was if they were actually attacking it for some reason."

"It was lucky they were not flying at the carts on the course. That could have been real dangerous," Dr. Brown said.

Jody Stone said, "They didn't seem scared when Al Conner fired a shotgun in the air. They finally left when he started firing at them. It was crazy that's for sure."

"The course has had it share of weird happenings recently," Dr. Stone said as he sipped his beer and wondered what would be the cause of the recent animals attacks on the golf course?

As Sean and Alex were walking through the park, which was only about a mile from Alex's house, Sean said, "This is a great park. It has everything children need. There are several baseball fields, tennis courts, basketball courts, a swimming pool, playground stuff and even an ice skating building. It's quite something to say the least."

"It's a nice park for certain, but it doesn't get as much attention from children as it used to. Today it seems kids would rather play computer games or text each other rather than play outside. Times have changed that's is for sure," Alex said as they continued their walk through the park. "By the way Sean, how is your leg feeling as of late?"

"It feels pretty damn good and walking doesn't bother me at all. I'll be as good as new when I return to work. Coming to visit you was a very good move."

"I'm glad you recovered so quickly. All the beers we've had probably helped in your healing process."

At The Marsh bar most of the seats at the bar were full and one of the large tables as well. There was one Eagle fan, Rich Montana and only one Patriot fan Les, who was the husband of Tracey, who owned Tracey's Restaurant. Tracey was a Bill's fan. Carl Clapton was at the bar and was getting people to enter his usual Sunday football pool, which was a routine for him. Cody Wayne was busy preparing free food for his customers on Sunday football days, with the help of bartender Judy.

Melissa Travers and Penny Sullivan were both at the local golf course asking Al Conner questions about the strange attack by a group of crows, that flew at the clubhouse. Conner told them that the birds flew into some windows and made large cracks in the windows. The crows seemed to be flying against the windows on purpose and didn't leave until he fired several shots at them from his shotgun. No one was injured, but several people were scared. Conner said it was like that old Hitchcock movie, *The Birds*.

"I wonder why the animals around here are acting so out of character?" Penny asked Melissa.

"I'm not sure but I would like to check out a theory, but it would mean going into those woods on the edge of the golf course and to do that we would need some one with a weapon to come with us."

"What are you thinking Melissa?" Penny asked with a puzzled look on her face.

"Something is making the animals around here act in such a crazy manner and it has to be something in those woods where they live. Don't you agree?"

"You might be right. However, before we dare to go in there we need a person with a weapon just in case we get attacked. I'm going to call a friend of mine who is a hunter."

"Do you think he will come today, or should we plan to enter those woods tomorrow. Tomorrow might be better and we can dress better, because the shorts we are wearing might not be able to deal with thorn bushes and whatever else we might run into back there. I'll try to make arrangements for tomorrow morning. I'll call you when I find out the exact time."

"Sounds good to me. See you tomorrow."

"We are going to hold off on reporting about the crow attack until we investigate the woods to see if we find some answers back in there that might explain the other animal attacks. See you at some time tomorrow."

Sean and Alex walked into Abelli's and the place was quite filled with both football fans and people there for lunch. Abelli's had a large screen TV on a far wall and several TVs behind the bar. The majority of football fans were Steeler fans with some Bill's fans scattered about.

George was tending bar and waved to Alex and Sean, who both sat at two seats open at the bar and ordered Harp beers from George. Sean said to Alex, "No Giant fans in here I assume."

"No Giant fans that I know of anywhere that I have ever seen."

"That's what you get living out here in the sticks. It's all Steelers and Bill's."

"Well I know a few Browns fans but not that many with the way they have been losing over the past years,"Alex said as he waved to Karen Hecate and her boyfriend Adam, who were having lunch at a near-by table. He also waved to Dr. Steelman and her husband Jim, who was a very good artist. Dr. Steelman and Jim waved back, smiling.

"So we have a beer bet on the game and I have the Steelers and have to spot you seven points. Correct?"

"That's is correct Sean and if it ends tied due to the points I'm getting from you, we do *rock . . . paper . . . scissors* to see who wins the beer,"

Alex said with a laugh. "and we make that two out of three."

Sean raised his beer and toasted his friend in agreement. Alex then ordered two dozen chicken wings as the game was set to begin.

"One must have chicken wings when the Bills play. I mean after all chicken wings became famous thanks to Buffalo," Alex mentioned.

"I thought Buffalo was famous for losing four Super Bowls," Sean said, lightly punching Alex on the arm.

The game progressed into the second quarter with the Steelers ahead by the score of 17-10, until there was only under a minute left until the half ended. Buffalo had a forty yard field goal attempt and it sailed wide right. "Damn, how can you be a pro and miss a forty yarder?" Alex said in frustration.

Sean laughed and said, "Seems like they did that in a Super Bowl."

"Don't rub it in my friend. I would have been ahead if that field goal would have been good. As it stands now with the points given me, we are tied right now." The half ended and Sean and Alex finished their beers and said so long to the people around them and left to walk to The Marsh bar for the second half.

On the North Road Tracy James and his wife Lisa were riding along in Tracy's truck. They were talking about how their daughter had been getting several scholarship offers as she was one of the top golfers in the entire state, when, as they approached a big curve in the road, suddenly, a car pulled out of a dirt road from their left and pushed the truck over the side of the road and down a steep cliff. Tracy yelled, "Jump, get out, quick!" Both Tracy and Lisa jumped out of the truck as it continued to fall down the steep drop. The car that forced them off the road sped away. Tracy, crashed into a small tree as he jumped from the truck and Lisa fell into thick thorn bushes. Tracy's arm was bleeding and a bone pushed through his skin. His head was also bleeding.

In the car that forced the truck from the road and down the cliff, Kite said, "So much for those fuckers."

Willy laughed at the comment and said, "I knew those fuckers would be coming this way and have to round that curve with the big cliff. Now we need to ditch this car and get us another one."

"Where the hell are we staying tonight?" Kite asked.

"Let's get us another car and drive to some small shit town near by."

Bruce Bannon and Wanita Wallace were riding their Harley's down North Road when they stopped quickly as they saw two people they knew on the side of the road. Both of them appeared to be injured. Bruce and Wanita got off their bikes and went over to Lisa and Tracy.

"What happened to you two?" Bruce asked, concerned at the blood all over both Lisa and Tracy.

"Tracy's arm is badly broken and I think he has a concussion. I'm all cut from the thorns down there. Our truck was pushed off the road on purpose. We have to get Tracy to the hospital," Lisa stated in a tensed tone.

"There's no damn cell service here. We can put you on our bikes and take you to the hospital but I don't think Tracy can make it on the back of a bike," Wanita said.

Bruce said, "I'll drive down the road and flag down the first car or truck I see and get them up here. Take care of them Wanita." Bruce then sped off on his bike.

Wanita looked over the edge of the road and saw the truck on its side, with windows smashed out and a door torn completely off. She looked at Lisa and said, "You two are very lucky to be alive. Tracy will be Ok after his arm is fixed. It could have been a lot more worse."

"Why would some one do that to us?" Lisa asked.

Wanita answered, "I just don't know Lisa." Wanita then ripped part of her shirt and tied it around Tracy's head. She didn't want to touch the arm where a bone had pushed its way through the skin. Tracy was not saying anything and was quite dazed.

Within ten minutes, Bruce was back followed by a truck that stopped near the scene. Tracy and Lisa were helped inside the truck and it turned around and headed back to Marshton. Bruce and Wanita followed the truck on the way to the hospital.

At The Marsh bar, Sean and Alex were having a beer and Sean said, "I want photos of some of these signs in here to take back to the city with me. Do you think the owner would mind?"

"Go ahead and take all the pictures you want. Cody won't care," Alex answered.

Sean took photos of a sign that had a picture of a 45 pistol with the words, *We don't call 911.* He also took several more photos and had Alex take a picture of him by a full sized poster of John Wayne. Cody Wayne bought Sean and Alex beers and shook Sean's hand for what he did to stop a terrorist attack, as did others in the bar. Several chips for beer were bought by other customers and given to Sean and Alex.

Sean and Alex posed in a group picture with everyone in the bar and Sean thanked everyone for the drinks and then Sean bought everyone in the bar a drink in return for their kindness.

The second half of the game went back and forth and with the fourth quarter starting the score was 31-24 with the Steelers leading. Cody Wayne sang his famous Steeler fight song and the crowd in the bar clapped and Sean had tears in his eyes from laughing. He leaned over to Alex and said, "This is the most fun I've had in a long time. This bar and the people here are great."

"It's a special place and that's why I always stop here on my walk home. The people who come here are what this country is all about or should be all about," Alex stated.

The game ended with the score, 38-30 Steelers. "You won by a lousy point. That missed field goal in the first half cost me the win with the seven points you gave me," Alex said.

"As they say, a win is a win," Sean said toasting his friend.

And hour later Sean and Alex left the bar and began their walk to Alex's house.

When Sean and Alex reached Alex's house Jesse and Jeanene were on the patio having glasses of wine. Jesse said,"Well it looks like they can still walk pretty straight and not stagger. They do look happy."

"Yes they certainly do," Jeanene replied.

"Well did you have a nice shopping adventure in Erie?" Alex asked.

"We had a fantastic time and lunch was terrific also," Jeanene answered.

"We also had a fantastic time doing our football thing," Sean said as he kissed his wife.

At the Marshton hospital, Lisa and Tracy were treated for their injuries. Tracy's broken arm was set and placed into a cast and he was to remain in the hospital overnight. Lisa was treated for cuts and bruises and released. Wanita helped Lisa with her phone call to the police telling them about the hit and run attack and the location of where it happened. The police said that they would remove any valuables and documents from the truck and call a towing company to see if the truck could be pulled out of the steep cliff.

Lisa thanked the police after relating the details she remembered from the incident. She said that she would come down to the station in the morning and so would Tracy if he was recovered enough. Lisa called a friend for a ride home after she checked on her husband.

Lisa also thanked Wanita and Bruce for all that they did.

At a small motel near an area located twenty miles from Marshton, Kite and Willy were eating pizza and Willy said, "Well we got us another car that isn't hot yet and we did good work on getting more revenge for my brother."

"What's left to do now?" Kite asked.

"I'm not sure yet but I need to think about it."

"Don't you think we've done enough to avenge your brother?"

"Maybe, but like I said I need to think on it."

"We have been lucky so far and if we keep fucking around we are going to get caught."

"Are you turning chicken shit on me?"

"No, but . . . whatever."

"Relax for tonight. Do a line and chill out baby."

A fire was blazing in Alex's fire pit and it was a clear sky with stars appearing overhead. Sean and Jesse had made an invitation for Alex and Jeanene to visit them in New York City over Christmas vacation.

"That sounds great. I haven't been to the city in a long time," Jeanene said.

"It would be nice to visit some of my old stomping grounds again,"Alex said.

"Then it's a done deal," Sean said.

The rest of the night was spent talking about what it was going to be like for Sean to return to duty and how Jesse would be up to her ears in law cases when she returned. They all went to bed around midnight.

CHAPTER 13

Unexpected Attack

Melissa Travers got a phone call from Penny Sullivan in the early morning, "I'm sorry Melissa but Mayor La Clare wants to meet with me this morning about some of the problems the city council has been having regarding several issues. I won't be able to go into the woods with you, but I did contact a friend who will go with you. His name is Jeff Bayern and he knows his way around the woods. He agreed to meet you at Tracey's Restaurant for breakfast and then go to the woods."

"That will be fine. Sorry you can't go with us. What time are we to meet?"

"I told him to meet you at nine this morning, if that is ok with you?"

"That sounds good to me. Good luck with the mayor."

"Thanks and I'll talk to you later. Good luck to you on your adventure. Be careful in there."

"Talk with you later." Melissa ended the call and went to her shower.

At 8:30, Jeff Bayern put his twelve gauge shotgun into his truck and several shells into a vest pocket. He really didn't expect to actually do any shooting. He also set a hunting knife on the seat next to his vest. He then drove to Tracey's to meet Melissa.

During breakfast Melissa talked with Jeff about why she wanted to check the woods that were located in the area behind the golf course. Jeff told her that those woods go a long way back and cross over to New York State. He told her that there was a small dirt road a mile down the road from the golf course that entered the woods. He could go down the dirt road a ways and then park.

Melissa said, "I want to see what is causing these animals to act so out of their norm. Something in those woods must be the cause."

"Well, are you ready to go and try to find out what could be in there to cause the animals to go nuts?"

"As ready as I ever will be." They left Tracey's and Melissa said,

"I'll park my car at the office and ride with you."

"I will follow you over there," Jeff said.

An hour later Jeff parked his truck on the dirt road as far as he could drive it down the road as the road ended and turned into just a small pathway. Melissa and Jeff got out of the truck and Jeff put on his vest and loaded his gun. He had a 22 caliber pistol but left it in his truck. The weather was warm with just a few clouds in the sky. Jeff said, "We can walk in the direction toward the woods a mile or so behind the golf course. There is a stream in there and a small pond. I've been back there when I was hunting in here a couple of times in the past. It is a good walk to get there."

"You are the guide. I've never been in here before. I'll follow you."

"Ok, let's see what we can find," Jeff said as he started off into the woods with Melissa behind him. The woods were fairly thick with a great many thorn bushes in the undergrowth.

After walking for around thirty minutes, they came into a small clearing. Jeff pointed in front of him at a small stream and up the stream Melissa could see a pond. There were several trees around the clearing. They both walked in the direction of the stream. They stopped when they heard several crows land in the near-by trees. "Where the hell did they come from?" Jeff said as he looked up at the crows."

"What is that beside the stream?" Melissa said looking at what looked like a pouch or backpack on the edge of the stream.

Jeff started to walk over to the object near the stream when suddenly out of the woods several coyotes came running toward Melissa and Jeff.

Jeff quickly raised his gun and fired at the coyotes. He yelled, "Melissa get up a tree . . . quick!"

Jeff fired and had killed two coyotes but the others kept coming. One coyote jumped at Jeff and bit his arm. Jeff shook the coyote off him. He then ran for a tree, but another coyote had ahold of his leg. He made a move to swing his gun the the coyote but the gun struck the tree he was near and the gun broke apart. The stock separating from the barrel. Jeff kicked the coyote off his leg and was able to swing up into the tree.

Melissa made it safely into a tree that had a low branch that she was able to reach and pull herself up into the tree.

Her backpack had fallen to the ground under the tree where a coyote had begun ripping it apart.

Jeff was in a tree about around ten feet away. Both his arm and leg were bleeding. His arm was the worst of the two.

Melissa yelled from her tree, "Jeff what are we going to do?"

Jeff looked over at Melissa and said, "Stay right where you are. Let me stop the bleeding in my arm first."

Melissa looked down at the coyotes. Some were jumping up the the bottom of the trees that Jeff and her were in but they couldn't reach either of the limbs Jeff or Melissa were on.

"Do you have your phone Melissa?" Jeff called over to her.

"My phone is in my backpack down on the ground and the coyotes have ripped it apart. I don't know if my phone is still in one piece."

"Shit. I left mine in my truck. My gun is broke in half. At least right now we're ok."

"Do you think these animals will leave any time soon?"

"Can't count on that. We have to figure a way out but I'm not sure just how."

Penny Sullivan tried to call Melissa after her meeting ended with the mayor but got no answer. She also tried to reach Jeff, but again got no answer. She became very worried. She waited for fifteen minutes and tried to reach both of them once again but no answer. She then sent text messages but got no response back. Penny then called Norm Smithson and told him the situation. Norm told Penny to track Melissa's smart phone with the GPS locator in her phone but got no location. Penny drove to the police station and met with the chief. He was able to track the GPS in Jeff's truck to the location where it was. Norm got one of his officers and with Penny the three of them started to drive to where Jeff's truck was located.

Jeff's arm was giving him a massive amount of pain as was his leg. He yelled over to Melissa, "I'm going to toss you my lighter and you can use your shirt to start signal fire. Take your shirt off and light it. Then toss it unto that pile of dry leaves and branches under that tree near you."

"What if I drop the lighter when you toss it to me?"

"Use you shirt to catch it in. Now take off your shirt."

Melissa thought to herself, of all days not to wear a bra. She removed her shirt and spread it out in front of her, ready to catch the lighter Jeff was going to throw to her.

"Are you ready?"

"Go ahead and throw it."

Jeff lightly tossed the lighter to Melissa and it landed in her spread out shirt. "Beautiful catch Melissa. Now be careful and go ahead and light your shirt. Roll it up into a ball first."

Melissa rolled her shirt up and held the Zippo lighter against the shirt until it started to burn. She then tossed it under the tree that was next to the tree she was in. In a short time a small fire started in the pile of leaves and branches and smoke rose.

Norm, Penny and Officer Smith got out of the police cruiser behind Jeff's truck. "There's no sign of them. Why the hell didn't Melissa answer her phone?" Norm asked.

"I don't know but I know why Jeff didn't. His phone is on his seat inside," Penny said as she looked inside the truck window.

Officer Smith asked, "How do we go about finding where they are?"

"I guess we try to see which direction they went," Norm said.

Penny looked up at the sky in front of her and saw smoke rising above the forest. "Look in that direction," she said pointing at the smoke. Norm and Officer Smith got shotguns from the police car and with Penny started off in the direction of the smoke.

From her tree Melissa saw a coyote go over to the object at the edge of the stream and dig into it. The coyote then spun around in circles and fell onto its side and then got up again and spin in a circle. She also saw several crows fly in the direction of the pond and then fly in all kinds of weird directions. The smoke from the fire she had started was starting to fade as the fire was going out. She yelled over to Jeff, "The fire is starting to die out. Now what?"

Jeff didn't want to say it but thought about having Melissa use her pants to set on fire in order to keep the fire going. "There is still smoke from the fire. Just wait a bit."

Melissa's bare chest was itching from the scratches she had got from climbing the tree and she had a cut on her face. However, she now knew why the animals were acting so crazy around the area and it had to do with the stream and the pond. The question is would she live to tell anyone about it?

Jeff and Melissa heard the sound of shots being fired in the surrounding woods and the coyotes started to run in that direction. More shots were fired and three coyotes ran back into the clearing and ran away into the woods over the stream. Then Melissa saw three figures walk into the clearing. "Thank heavens!" she said out loud.

Both Jeff and Melissa started to climb down from the trees they were in. Penny Sullivan looked at Melissa's bare chest and said, "Were you doing a strip tease in that tree?"

"Ha Ha, very funny. Now give me something to cover up with if you don't mind."

Penny gave Melissa her sweat shirt and said, "I was so worried about you. I'm glad you are alive!"

Norm said to Jeff, "We have to get you to the hospital. Let Smitty here bandage your arm. We brought a small first aid kit with us."

"I need a bandage on my leg too. Those damn coyotes did a number on me. My shotgun's been busted in half. How many of those bastards did you kill? I heard the shooting."

"Several of them back there. They came right at us," Norm said.

Melissa explained to Penny why the coyotes and other animals were acting so crazy as they both looked down at the backpack on the ground by the stream. "Look at the remains inside the backpack and along the edge of the stream. Drugs of some sort," Melissa stated.

"You're right. Norm look over here," Penny said.

"Where did this shit come from?" Norm said.

"You better get somebody up here to check that pond too," Melissa said.

"We have to get Jeff out of here and to the hospital. I radioed in for an ambulance to meet us at the golf course parking lot. I'll have this area cleared by troopers. Let get the hell out of here," Norm said.

"Very good idea," Melissa said.

On the way back to where Jeff's truck was parked Melissa related to Penny Sullivan all that happened to her and Jeff.

Finally, when they reached the dirt road where the police car and Jeff's truck were parked, Penny Sullivan gave Melissa a kiss on the cheek and a hug. "I'm so thankful that you and Jeff survived this ordeal."

"Officer Smith will drive your truck home for you. Your wife will be contacted to meet you at the hospital. Smitty will take your truck to your house and get a ride back into town. On the way to meet the ambulance Penny and Melissa sat in the front with the chief and Jeff was in the back seat so he would have more room.

After Jeff Bayern was checked into the hospital and treated by Dr. Steelman and Melissa was treated for her cut on her face, Chief Smithson, Penny Sullivan and Melissa left the hospital. Jeff was to remain over night. Penny and Melissa went to the paper's office and Chief Smithson went to his headquarters to contact Captain Mason. The chief related to the captain about the events the happened in the woods and told him about the drugs found along the stream and the probability that more drugs were in the small pond by the way crows had been seen flying in crazy directions and about how crows basically attacked the clubhouse on the golf course. Mason wrote down the location of the stream and told Smithson that he would send troopers to the area and would contact the DEA for assistance in processing the area.

Penny Sullivan and Melissa talked about the story they were going to write about today's adventure in the woods and the coyote attack. An hour later the story was ready to go to print.

Mystery of Recent Animal Attacks . . . Solved.

Thanks to the deductive reasoning of reporter, Melissa Travers, the mystery of the animal attacks in the local woods and on the local golf course has been solved. Melissa and local resident, Jeff Bayern, entered the woods a few miles in the rear of the golf course in search of the cause of the dangerous attacks.

Melissa and Jeff were attacked by coyotes while con—ducting their search for answers. Jeff was bitten twice by the enraged coyotes, after shooting some of the them.

Melissa and Jeff managed to climb into trees in order to escape the coyotes. Only by creative thinking by Jeff and Melissa enabled them to be rescued. Jeff tossed a lighter to Melissa from the tree he was in and Melissa started her shirt on fire and threw it into a pile of dry leaves and branches to cause a small fire to ignite.

Smoke was seen by searchers looking for Melissa and Jeff. The searchers were led by Chief Smithson, Officer Smith and Penny Sullivan. Chief Smithson and Officer Smith had to kill several coyotes on the way to the scene where Melissa and Jeff were trapped.

Once the scene was secured, a variety of drugs were found lining the edge of a stream and it was suspected that more drugs were in a near-by pond. How the drugs got to the location is not yet certain but an investigation is underway. We do know that animals were eating the drugs and that is what caused them make their attacks.

The community of Marshton can be thankful for the courage of Melissa Travers and Jeff Bayern; for they brought an end the mystery of why animals were acting out of the norm and attacking residents. Hopefully, who—ever was responsible for putting the drugs into the stream and pond will soon be arrested by authorities.

The story also had several photos on the front page of the Melissa and Jeff in the trees and of the dead coyotes and of the drugs lining the edge of the stream. The photos were taken by Penny Sullivan when she first arrived on the scene. (Melissa had covered her chest with her arms when Penny took the photo of her in the tree.)

Before Melissa left the office she said to Penny, "You know I'm going to need a new phone don't you, because mine was chewed to pieces by those damn coyotes."

"That's the least I can do for you. Besides getting a new phone, you have earned a nice raise in pay, because it was your theory that answered the mystery of the animal attacks. Super work Melissa. Penny then gave her star reporter a hug.

Chief Smithson met with Darlene La Clare and informed her of what took place in the woods and how the mystery of why animals were attacking in different locations was now solved. The mayor said, "Finally, things might get back to normal around here."

"We still need to know how those drugs got in the woods and into the stream and pond. Captain Mason and the DEA will be leading the investigation."

"Well, nice job Norm."

"I thank you, but Melissa Travers actually figured it out."

"Yes, she is quite the fine reporter."

CHAPTER 14

Clues

On Tuesday morning Alex handed the daily paper over to Sean and said, "That coyote attack was quite something. People are lucky to have escaped."

"I read the article and to think that drugs were what the cause was for making the animals attack. Now the key is to get rid of the drugs back in the woods and find out how they got there in the first place."

Jesse took the paper from Sean and started to read the article on the attack in the woods. After a short time she said, "Well at least now it is clear why the animals in the woods attacked in the first place. Who would have expected that drugs would be the cause of the attacks. I wonder if the drugs were put there on purpose?"

"That's a good question Jesse and perhaps we will find out more today after Sean meets with Captain Mason and Chief Smithson."

Sean took a sip of his coffee and then said, "That meeting should be interesting. I wonder what information they have that the public doesn't know about?"

"Maybe you will find out at noon today," Alex stated.

Several hours later an unmarked car pulled into Alex's driveway and Chief Smithson and Captain Mason got out of the car. Alex introduced Sean and Jesse to the men and took them out on the patio. After a few minutes Alex and Jesse went into the house and Sean, Mason and Smithson sat around the patio table.

Captain Mason spoke first, "The reason for wanting this meeting with you is to get your professional opinion on the facts and details of the case of the murders in the woods and in the motel room where the supposed killer, killed himself." Mason then opened a thick folder and showed Sean photos from the various crime scenes.

Sean looked at each photo very carefully. "Ok, the first killing in the woods shows a victim hanging from a tree with his penis cut off and skin cut from his upper body. Now to me that shows both rage and revenge, possibly as motives. The killer was still in the immediate area as shots were fired at the guy who happened upon the scene. Isn't that correct?"

"Yes it is right and we recovered a bullet from the atv that was fired at. We were not able to get any prints from the crime scene," Mason said as he put the next few photos in front of Sean which were from the crime scene where his troopers were killed along with a man attached to a tree with his penis stuffed into his mouth. "Now we got no prints from this crime scene either. This is another reason I'm here, to get justice for my two dead men."

Sean spent several minutes in a study of the photos in front of him.

"These are grusome to say the least. I'm so sorry for your loss of the two brave troopers. Now, you say the troopers were both shot in the back and in the head?"

"That's correct."

"What about footprints at the scene?"

"There were none to mention, just some drag marks where it appeared that the two troopers were pulled under the tree where the dead man was attached," Mason said in a low voice.

"So correct me if I'm wrong, but the troopers were shot in the back and afterwords, shot in the head; which means they were surprised from the rear by a killer. Now to me that is most unlike officers to be shot from behind when checking out a crime scene. Usually, you make certain your back is protected first before going forward. We are trained to do that."

"My troopers are also trained to do that, so it is a mystery as to how this happened," Mason said.

"You know shit can happen where mistakes are made, but in this case I would say the troopers would have checked the camp out first and then have gone out back. So either they missed a killer inside or else they were set up by a killer who was inside and directed the troopers outside where they were then shot in their backs by the killer who directed them to go outside. Now who do you think officers would leave in their rear not fearing . . . a man or a woman?" Sean asked.

"You think they left a woman inside who then shot them in the back Sean?" Mason asked in a confused tone.

"I think it's very possible and it has happened to some officers in the city. Trust can often kill you and it's better to trust no one at a crime scene. There just could be more than one killer here. Think about it who is more apt to cut off a man's dick . . . a man or a woman. In two crime scenes a penis was cut from a body."

"Damn Sean, you could be right about that fact," Chief Smithson said.

"You also said that the bodies of the troopers looked to have been pulled under the tree where another victim was attached. Well, again that points to two killers, because a woman would have a hard time pulling two big men under a tree and besides after the killings, whoever did them would want to get away from the scene quickly,"Sean said.

"I definately tend to agree with you Sean. Now what makes me think that this case should not have been closed is the motel crime scene. This scene looks like it was staged to me. Here are the photos from the scene." Mason then spread the motel crime scene photos in front of Sean.

Once again, Sean looked at all of the photos from the motel crime scene and at the note left by the man who confessed to the killings in the woods. Sean was surprised to see that the man had said that his male lover was killed because of meth use; which flipped Sean's mind to the article he had read this morning about drugs in the woods where the coyote attack had just happened. Captain Mason went through all of the doubts he had about the crime scene and then asked Sean how he felt about the scene.

"I've seen my share of killings in the city for sure. Most were straight up murders of victims, but some were self-inflicted and the self-inflicted ones are tricky because they can be set to look like a person offed themself. However, you have to be careful to check those out to try and leave no doubt that the person really did kill themself."

"I have my doubts about this and that's another reason why I want your take on this scene," Mason said.

"It's one thing to look at an actual crime scene and quite another to try and read things from photos. I'll give it my best attempt anyway."

Sean then looked at the photos again. After a few minutes Sean said, "I will give you a list of things to check out.

1. Was the guy on the bed who killed himself, right or left handed? This was made to look like he was right handed. That is because the usual case is when some person pulls a trigger, they use their dominant hand.
2. The blood splatter on the wall has a pattern where there is a tell in most cases. The head usually goes left or right when it self-inflicted. and so does the splatter pattern. A set-up would be straight.
3. If any bits of plastic were found near the splatter, it could have come from a plastic bottle that had been used as a silencer, which could mean it was a set up, because most self-inflicted shooters couldn't give a damn who hears the shot.
4. The note left behind should be checked by a pro who can normally tell if the vic wrote it or not when comparing samples of the writing."

"That's a hell of a lot to check into and I'll have to do it on the sly because the case has been closed by a regional commander," Mason stated.

"That is up to you captain, of course. I'd do it if I were you,"Sean said.

Chief Smithson said, "I'd do it. You can count on me to help you on the sly."

"Look. let me say a few more things that might help, which you probably know, but anyway, if it was indeed a set up, then the real killers are out there somewhere. Now you have to nail the fuckers.

So,

1. I would check all cars that have been stolen in the area.
2. Check motels in the area for people who were there when cars were ripped off.
3. You have that note left at the motel scene. You can compare it with the registers at the motels. It's a shot in the dark, but why not.
4. The real killers have to have motives for what they are doing if this whole thing was a set up. What in hell could it be?
5. It's got to be A. Just for the plain hell of it.

B. A revenge factor of some sort.

C. Some gang related shit of some kind.

Now, what's been happening around here as of late that normally isn't happening?"

Chief Smithson thought a minute and said, "Well, a couple of fires, but we get those now and then."

"What burned?" Sean asked.

The chief replied, "We had a truck fire at the fire hall off of North Road. Then there was a fire at JK's Tavern, that was arson. There was a drug OD, but we get a few of them every month now days. Oh yeah, then there was a rattlesnake that was in a guy's truck that bit him. Then there was a car that pushed a truck off the road and down a cliff."

"The fires I can see as happening as a routine now and then, but a snake in a truck and a hit and run where a truck was pushed off a cliff, now those are out of the routine," Sean said.

"I didn't here about the snake in the truck Norm," Mason said.

"Yeah, it happened to Mike Mayer."

"How did he say the snake got into his truck?" Sean asked.

"I don't think any person asked him how," the chief answered.

"Those signs point to a revenge factor. See who is pissed at those who were injured. At this point, even those harmed by the loss suffered in the fires. You need strings to pull to find these killers. I'd say you have some," Sean said.

Captain Mason stood up with Chief Smithson and both men thanked Sean. Alex and Jesse came out of the house and were also thanked by Mason and Smithson. After the captain and chief left Alex and Jesse sat at the patio table. Sean and Alex had a beer and Jesse had a bottle of mineral water. Sean related what he had found out while the meeting had taken place and that the ending of the case could have been closed too soon.

CHAPTER 15

A Guest?

Chief Smithson and Captain Mason left Alex's house and went to the office of the chief. They began talking about the details that Sean related to them. Mason said, "At least we know where the drugs came from that made the animals attack. The meth came from the guy who offed himself in the motel. At least we think it came from him being fucked up on the stuff and he killed his lover according to that note we found."

"Well like Sean said, are we certain that he wrote the note? It very well could be another person wrote the note and pointed all the blame for the killings onto the dead guy on the bed," Smithson related.

"Sean spoke of a woman who may have killed my two troopers at the cabin crime scene. It does make sense that it could have happened. In that case we have more than one killer out there."

"What in hell is the motive behind all of this? Sean gave us a revenge factor that could be behind the killings and what could be the damn tie-in for revenge?" the chief questioned.

"Shit, we have the fires, the killings in the woods, the drugs along the stream that caused the animal attacks, the hit and run, the OD you mentioned, and even the fucking snake attack. Now what could tie all that together?" Mason said as he scratched his head in wonder. "and as I said we have the death in the motel room that looked staged to me."

"I think we need a little time to process all of the information and try to come up with a tie-in. Let's both think on it for a day and get back to each other tomorrow. I know you and your troopers at busy dealing with the drugs at the stream and the pond and testing the dead coyotes for drugs in their systems."

"Yes, that's a good idea right now. Hell, they are draining the pond and warning all of the cabin owners to avoid all water coming from the stream until it has been tested and made sure that no drugs remain in the water. It's quite a cluster fuck out there."

"At least you have the boys and girls from the DEA to help you out," the chief said with a laugh.

Captain Mason stood up and said, "I'll give you a call tomorrow.

Now I am on my way out to play with the DEA folks. They hired a couple of guys to cut a path into the stream so they wouldn't get scratched walking in to the site. The DEA are real outdoors people," Mason said with a laugh.

Willy walked outside the Marshton Post Office and got into the car that Kite was behind the wheel of and said, "Well I found out that the guy Denny James is having his mail held because he is on some damn safari in Africa, if you can believe that. They gave that information because I said I was a friend of his from out of town and couldn't reach him. It looks like Mr. James just got lucky. I hope a rhino kills the bastard. They also told me that he isn't expected back for some time."

"Where do we go now? Can't we get the fuck of this town at last?"

"Not quite yet. Drive to Salamanca again for tonight. We will stay at a different motel."

"You know we are pushing our luck driving ripped off cars and staying around here," Kite said.

"Don't fuckin' worry about it. Just drive."

Sean and Jesse wanted to take Alex and Jeanene out for an early dinner. Both Alex and Jeanene had early evening classes that they taught and the plan was to meet Sean and Jesse at Abelli's at 7:30pm.

In the meantime Sean and Jesse had packed most of their clothes and got ready to leave Marshton tomorrow and head back to New York. They had rented a car and planned to drive back to the city tomorrow.

Sean had told Jesse that his leg was feeling great and the trip back to the city wouldn't bother his leg and he was looking forward to getting back to their own place. Jesse agreed on that fact after being away for nearly a month. Jesse and Sean left Alex's house and walked down to the small creek near Alex's house. Jesse said, "This is a very relaxing environment here. It will be quite a difference when we get back to the city."

"That's for sure my dear. It has been a great place to spend time while my leg healed. It really feels back to normal again."

"Are you sure you are ready to go back to work fulltime?" Jesse asked.

"Yes I am. I got several texts from my captain asking me the same question."

"I just hope you are sure."

Just then, Sean's phone rang and Sean looked very surprised as he spoke into his phone, "Well yes I could do that if you are sure that it would be okay with the troopers? Oh, well in that case I will do it on the sly as long as Captain Mason is also doing it on the sly. I mean the case has been closed by his superior commander and I know the captain doesn't feel that the real killer or killers have been caught."

Sean's captain said, "I spoke with Investigator Isabelle Clarkson, who I have met several times and she would consider it a personal favor if you were to give Captain Mason a helping hand on the investigation, which he is conducting without his commander's knowledge, because he wants justice for his two dead troopers. I will take care of details here so you will be extended additional leave time. Sean, you would be doing me a favor by helping out up there."

Sean looked at his wife and then said, "I will do what I can to help Captain Mason, if you are sure you want me to remain here for a time."

"Yes, I do want you to be involved, but we'll keep that between you and me for the time being. Captain Mason and Isabelle Clarkson will also be in the know about your involvement."

"My wife will have to make arrangements with her law firm, but I'm sure she can make arrangements for a little longer stay up here in God's country. My friend won't mind if we stay a bit longer at his house. So I'll keep you informed about what's going on with the on the sly investigation."

"Thanks a bundle Sean. I hope you find the true killers. Talk to you soon."

Sean looked at Jesse and said, "My captain has been contacted by a special investigator from the state police and asked my captain if I could remain here for a time to help with the investigation into the killings, which has been closed by the commander of the state police and is still going on behind the scenes by Captain Mason. So do you think you can get some additional time away from your job?"

Jesse shook her head and said, "Wow! To say the least. I'll have to call my office and find out about more time away. I guess it will depend on if any big cases are on the table. Let's go back to Alex's and I will call the firm."

Kite and Willy checked into a motel that they hadn't been to before once inside their room, Willy said, "What do you say about getting out your *fuck me dress and pretty panties*?"

"What do you have in mind?"

"I thought we would go to the casino and you could lure some sucker out of the casino and back to the room so we could have some playtime tonight," Willy said with a smile.

Kite smiled and said, "What are we going to do with our playtime guest after we are done with him?"

"The same thing we do with all our guests. We fix a hot fix for him and then get rid of him where it will look like he ODed himself."

"You know there's cameras all over the fucking place in those casinos," Kite related.

"I know, I know. So you will be careful and after you hook the guy, you say that you have to pee and will meet him outside, where it will be dark near a side entrance. You let the guy drive you back here and I'll follow you back. Once you get him inside the room, you know what to do."

"Yes I know what to do. It's not like I haven't done it before. I'll try to get some guy with some coins."

"Just do your thing and I'll be watching from a distance."

Later that night at Abelli's Jesse and Sean were seated at a table when Jeanene and Alex walked inside and immediately came over to the table and sat down. "So, what's new with the two New Yorkers?" Alex asked.

Sean looked at his wife and they both looked at Alex as Sean answered, "Well my friend, as the old saying goes, *The best laid plans of mice and men . . . .*,What I'm saying is the changes are definitely afoot."

"What exactly are you talking about Sean?" Alex asked puzzled.

"Well, how would you like some roomies for a little longer?" Sean said.

"Now what in hell is going on here Sean?" Alex said as the drink orders came to the table.

Jesse looked at Alex and said, "Perhaps you should have a taste of that beer before Sean tells you what is going on."

Alex looked at Jeanene, who also looked very confused at the conversation. Alex took a long sip of his beer and then said, "Okay, now tell me Sean."

"This stays between those of us at this table, but I have been asked by my captain in New York to remain here for a time and help Captain Mason with an investigation that is going to be conducted without Mason's commander knowing about it, because that commander has closed the case. So can Jesse and I remain as your guests for a time longer?"

Alex looked at Sean and Jesse and said, "Of course you can stay as long as you want, but what is going down with the investigation, that your captain in New York wants you involved?"

Sean answered, "It seems that my captain knows a special investigator named Isabelle Clarkson with the Pennsylvania State Troopers, who agrees with Captain Mason that the real killers have not been caught and wants to continue the investigation with my help. So my captain is arranging for me to stay here for a short time period and it all has to be done on the sly. I know it's confusing."

Jesse said, "My law firm stated that since you have a fax machine Alex, I can get the prelim details on a case that will be going to court in a month, so I can work from your house. That is if it's is all right with you Alex?"

"You know it will be fine with me Jesse. Actually, I'm happy you are both able to stay longer. This calls for another round of drinks before we order dinner," Alex said with a smile.

"I'm also glad you can stay Jesse. Perhaps you can visit me at the college and I'll give you the personal tour," Jeanene said.

"Sounds great Jeanene," Jesse said.

The waitress came to take the dinner orders. Jeanene ordered Veal Parmigiana, Alex ordered Veal Scaloppini, Jesse ordered Fettuccini Terra E Mare and Sean ordered a NY Strip Steak. Jeanene also ordered a bottle of Chardonnay for herself and Jesse. Both Alex and Sean ordered a beer.

Laurie, the waitress, took the order and left to place their order and get the drinks. Alex said to Sean, "So you couldn't wait to return to New York. That's why you passed on the great Italian food and went with the NY steak?"

"I missed my favorite steak and the city too," Sean answered.

Jesse said, "Sean most always orders his favorite food, steak."

"I did order spaghetti on the side just so I would keep in the Italian mode like the rest of you."

"How sweet of you dear," Jesse replied.

"This chef, Deano and his assistant chef, Valerine are really great and that is why this place is always crowded. People come from all around to eat here. Carla and George have a gold mine here," Alex said.

"What exactly is it that you ordered Jesse?" Jeanene asked.

"It consists of chicken, shrimp and mushrooms. It just has a fancy name," Jesse answered.

At the casino, Kite was at one of the bars sipping a glass of wine and was being eyed by a man who looked to be around fifty. He was two seats away from Kite. She made eye contact with him several times and turned in her seat as she let a napkin fall under her seat. As she turned she spread her legs so the man two seats away could get a look at her panties as she bent down to get the napkin. In a short time the man moved to the seat next to her and said, "Allow me to get your next drink for you. I'm alone and I see that you are too. Maybe we can have a conversation?"

Kite smiled at him and said, "I am alone tonight. My girlfriend is coming down from Buffalo tomorrow. I am staying at the motel we rented for the next few days and decided to come to the casino to entertain myself tonight."

The man introduced himself to Kite. He stated that his name was John and he was from Erie, Pennsylvania. Kite told him her name was Sherry and thanked him for the drink. The man said that he was a salesman and often stopped at this casino. He also said that he was divorced without any children. The guy named John also told Kite that he had just won over $5,000 on a slot machine and felt lucky.

Kite smiled at what the man told her. She said, "I didn't have any luck with the slots. I am lucky to have met you however."

The man smiled at Kite and said, "No, it's me who is lucky to have met you. Can I get you another drink?"

Kite agreed and this time ordered a whiskey and ginger. John, switched his drink order from a beer to a Jack and coke. Kite let her dress pull up on her legs so when she turned in her seat to face the man named John, that he could just barely see her pink panties. She could see a rise in his pants and smiled.

After two more drinks each, Kite said to John, "I think I should be going because I feel a little buzzed."

John said, "Where is your motel?"

"Not that far from here. I took a cab over to the casino," Kite answered.

"I'd be glad to give you a ride to your motel. My car is in the back parking lot."

"That would be so nice of you. I have some whiskey in my room. You can come in and have a drink for giving me ride."

"Sounds good to me. Ready to go?"

"I have to use the ladies room and get my coat. I'll meet you out by the shuttle stop near the side entrance. See you soon." Kite got up and left and the man walked in the direction of the side entrance and was thinking that he might get laid tonight with a younger and good looking woman. He had a smile on his face.

Willy, who watched Kite's action at the bar left the casino and drove back to the motel room before Kite and her guest arrived. Willy got into the bathroom and held a gun in his hand. Within ten minutes, Kite and her guest walked into the motel room. Kite kissed her guest and turned his back to the bathroom. Suddenly, Willy was behind the man named John, with a gun pointed at the back of John's head.

"What the hell's going on?" John said.

"Do what you are told and you won't get hurt. Now get your ass on the bed," Willy said.

"Is this a fucking set-up or something?" John asked.

"Shut the fuck up and listen. Get on the bed. Lay on your stomach," Willy said to the man. John did as he was told and Kite attached each one of his hands to the bed posts. Willy got a roll of tape and taped the man's mouth. Kite began taking the man's clothes off, until the man was totally naked. Willy looked in the man's wallet and pulled out a big wad of bills. "Nice work baby," Willy said holding up the bills in his hand.

"Yes, it was and it all went according to the plan. This guy was a real sucker for the dress and pink panties. I think he thought he was going to fuck me but now is he in for a surprise or what?" Kite said before going into the bathroom. Willy tied each one of their guest's legs to the bottom bed posts.

Kite came out of the bathroom, naked except for a dildo strapped around her. She then greased the dildo with KY jelly and mounted the man on the bed. She pushed in and out of him until she reached orgasm. She didn't care if the man under her did or not. Kite sat in a chair and had a drink while Willy counted the money from the man's wallet. He said to Kite, "Almost six grand here."

"Plus a free fuck for me. I think I'll fuck him once more for good measure before we split." Kite put the dildo back on and fucked their guest once again and again reached orgasm.

Willy fixed a loaded syringe and with a gloved hand and then stuck it into the guest's arm. He died almost immediately. Willy said to Kite, "Now we put this guy in his car and I drive it back to the casino and you follow me in the other car. I put the syringe in the guy's hand and we put a few hundred back in the guy's wallet. Make sure we wiped the car clean and off we go to a different motel in the good old state of Pennsylvania. Meanwhile our playmate died of an OD as far as the cops know. Killing can be so easy these days."

Around the fire pit in Alex's yard, Sean, Jesse, Jeanene and Alex were talking about what a good time they had at Abelli's and how nice it was that they would be able to spend more time together than was expected at the start of this day.

CHAPTER 16

On The Sly

The next day, behind an empty cabin in the woods, which was near an access road, Willy started a fire after breaking into the cabin an placing an explosive device into a metal container. The explosive device could be triggered by the cell phone call, much like the IED's used in Iraq and Afghanistan. A call was made to the volunteer fire department about the fire at the cabin. The call was made from a throw away phone made by Kite.

When the fire fighters arrived on the scene Willy watched from a distance, hidden by several thick trees. He was looking for the man directing the fire fighters. When he saw the man he was looking for walk near the cabin with other fire fighters, he called the cell phone number placed inside the explosive device inside the cabin, Instantly, a loud explosion echoed all around the woods and the cabin was blown apart. Several fire fighters were knocked off their feet and the man Willy was watching looked like he had been hit by flying shrapnel from objects that flew out from the explosion. Willy smiled and walked through the woods until he came out on a dirt road where Kite was in a car. Willy got inside the car and said, "Well that went good. I got the bastard I wanted to get plus a few more with him. You should have seen that blast."

Kite said, "I heard it from over here. Damn, it was loud. Was there any thing left of that cabin?"

"Not much that I could see. Let's get out of here before anyone comes up this road."

Kite drove off the dirt road and headed down the paved highway. She asked Willy, "Where are we going now?"

"We'll stay in some small motel near here and we have one more thing to accomplish before we leave the area for good."

"What exactly do we have to accomplish? Haven't you done what you set out to do in the first place?"

"Almost all that I wanted to do, but not quite all," Willy said with a grin. Kite asked Willy, "How in the fuck did you ever learn to make a bomb like that?"

"I told you before, you can learn a lot of shit online. You can make bombs outta almost anything. You can make one outta meth chemicals if you wanted to. You have to be careful or you'll blow your own ass up while making the bomb."

"You are fucking crazy fucking with bombs."

"Why thank you my dear," Willy said laughing.

"Can't we leave this place now? I'm sick of all these fucking woods."

"We are almost finished like I said. We'll relax for tonight," Willy said has he put his hand in between Kite's legs.

Penny Sullivan at her Marshton office and had just got off the phone. Penny looked at Melissa Travers and said, "That fire was really bad. Two men were injured and are in serious condition and two others are also injured, but not in serious condition. The call I got from one of the fire fighters at the scene said that a huge explosion from inside the cabin blew the injured men off their feet and shrapnel from the cabin flew in all directions. He said, they were lucky from the nature of the blast that more fire fighters were not hurt."

"Do we know the names of the injured yet?" Melissa asked.

"No names have been released yet, but how about you going to the scene of the fire and I will go to the hospital in an attempt to find out who was injured and what their condition is. See if you can find out what caused the explosion at that cabin and who owns the place. I'll meet you back here in a few hours," Penny said.

At Alex's house, Sean said to Jesse, "Captain Mason is coming by to talk about the case. I don't know how much I can really help to get justice for his two dead men since I haven't even seen any of the crime scenes, except by looking at photos and they don't give you an accurate account of the scene."

Jesse replied, "You can only do the best that you can. Your captain in the city wants you to help if you can. By the way, I am going to be busy on my computer getting information about the upcoming case I am going to be involved with soon. Thank goodness Alex happens to have a fax machine."

"Captain Mason will be here soon. We will meet out on the patio so we will not disturb your legal work. Jesse kissed Sean and walked into the room Alex used as an office. Sean sat around the patio table writing down notes that he wanted to talk about with Mason:

1. How was this investigation going to be kept out of the public's knowledge?

2. How was the captain going to keep his own troopers from knowing what he was up on his own?

3. What about people asking Alex why Sean and his wife were still in town?

4. What about two killers involved and not the guy found in the motel room?

5. Was there really a woman killer involved at the trooper's ambush?

6. He needed to find a motive or a link to the killings other than what was suspected currently.

7. He needed to actually visit the crime scenes even if they had been processed by the troopers.

8. If there are killers out there . . . where the hell are they staying?

9. There has to be some tie-in to what has been going on around the area, with crazy animal attacks caused by drugs located on the edge of the stream and in the pond. Who really put the drugs there and why?

10. Recent crimes in the area have to be checked out in terms of some related tie-in to the killings.

11. The first killing, where the vic was hanged from a tree and skin cut from the body was done from a rage or from some type of revenge.

It took a strong person or persons to hang the guy from a tree. Then cut off his dick after the fact. The second killing of the vic at the camp where the vic was nailed to a tree and his dick cut off represents rage or some type of sexual deal by a killer.

12. What about the trooper's weapons? Were all of them accounted for at the motel crime scene?

DavidClose

13. What info did the captain have from Ohio police about the guy in the motel room who offed himself, if indeed he did off himself?
14. What about the note that was left by the guy in the motel room?

Did he write it or did some one who killed him write it? Was it written by a woman or by a man. Right handed or left handed person who wrote the note?

15. Is Chief Smithson going to be part of the sly investigation? He could help by getting information about local crime tie-ins. When Penny Sullivan reached the hospital the parking lot it was packed with family members' cars of the injured fire fighters. Penny was able to find out the names of the injured by talking with family members. Two of the most seriously injured were Assistant Chief Reardon and fire fighter White. Two fire fighters with less serious injuries were fire fighter Passman and fire fighter Robbins. No one knew much information about what caused the injuries except that there was an explosion at the scene of the fire.

At the scene of the fire, Melissa Travers talked to some fire fighters, who were still in shock over the injuries of their fellow fire fighters and what caused such a large explosion. The fire inspector had not arrived at the scene as of yet. The head Fire Chief, Chip Cline, was out of town for a county fire meeting and was not available for a comment. Melissa did get various comments from several fire fighters as to what may have caused such a large explosion. The guesses ran from a propane tank that had a leak and blew up, to a kerosene heater

130

and cans of kerosene that may have been inside the cabin. No one knew for certain what exactly caused the explosion and the pieces of shrapnel that took down several fire fighters. All of the fire fighters felt lucky to still be alive.

When Captain Mason arrived at Alex's house, he came out to the patio where Sean stood and shook his hand. Sean offered him coffee or bottled water. Mason choose coffee and took a seat at the patio table. Sean brought out the two cups of coffee and joined Mason at the table.

Mason looked down at the notes that Sean had made and said, "I see you have been working on our private investigation."

"Speaking of keeping the investigation private, how do you plan to keep it private?" Sean asked.

"Well, I wish I could trust all my troopers to keep it private, but there are some who want to climb the ladder and would not be able to keep it private, if you know what I mean."

"Yes I do. It seems in every organization there are always assholes who cannot be trusted to keep a lid on things. So what are you going to do?"

"Well first of all, I took a week's vacation, starting today, so I won't have to be at headquarters. Now if we need computer info or research, we can use Chief Smithson's computers, which will let us into crime scene data, etc."

"That sounds good. Now I'd like to go over the notes I made with you because it will give me a better grasp on where things stand. But first, we both agree that the guy found dead in the motel most probably was not the actual killer . . . right?"

"Well, that's why we doing this on our own, If I didn't feel that the crime scene at the motel wasn't a set-up, I would not be here and on a week's vacation."

"Right then let me go down the list I made with you," Sean said.

When Sean finished going over the notes he had made with Captain Mason, he learned that the note left by the supposed killer in the motel room, was tested and there was no definite answer as to whether he wrote the note or didn't write it. The Ohio police didn't have much to offer from the arrest forms. Simply that the man was a known gay and had been arrested a few times, but nothing of a serious nature. There was nothing in the records if he was left handed or right handed.

When they finished talking over the notes that Sean had made Mason stood and streched saying, "Not a hell of a lot to go on is there?"

Sean looked up at the captain and said, "I'd like to visit the crime scenes just to get my own view of each site. I know they have been processed but it would help me, if you don't mind."

"Sure we can go now as the scenes have all been put to rest and the only place people will be around is the motel crime scene and I'll just bullshit whoever is working that you are some official of some sort who just wanted a look at the motel room."

"Great," Sean said and stood up. "Let me say goodbye to my wife and get a few things." Sean walked into the house and went into the bedroom and got his glock pistol and put it out of sight under a light jacket. He went into Alex's office and kissed his wife. He told her where he was going with Captain Mason.

Jesse said to him, "Be very careful out there Sean. There are woods out there and it isn't Central Park."

"I will and I'll see you in a few hours. Love you."

"I love you too so be careful out there dear."

Mason drove his personal car and not a state issued car so he would not easily be recognized if passed by a trooper's car."

Penny Sullivan and Melissa met at the paper's office to write the article about the fire and explosion.

After talking about the details to put into the article for a half an hour, they wrote the lead story for tomorrow's paper.

Fire and Explosion Injure Four Fighters

Sullivan . . . Travers . . . A fire and a terrific explosion at a cabin off North Road seriously injured two fire fighters and also injured two other fire fighters, with less serious injuries. From reports at the scene, a call came in about a fire at the cabin and when the fire fighters arrived at the scene and began to fight the fire, a huge explosion erupted, sending shrapnel in all directions and causing the injuries to four firemen. The cabin was destroyed.

The cause of the fire and the explosion has yet to be determined by the fire inspector who had not arrived at the scene at the time of the writing of this story. The names of the injured fire fighters will be released when all family members have been notified.

There were several photos of the fire scene taken by Melissa Travers and several interviews from the fire fighters who experienced the explosion.

As Captain Mason and Sean were riding to the spot where the first killing happened in the woods, Mason asked Sean how difficult it was to be a homicide detective in a large city like New York and from Sean he got the reply that certain crime scenes basically can solve the crime commited by the details left at the scene and others take a lot of leg work. It can be a damn hard task at times, but when a case is solved and you put some asshole behind bars, then it is very rewarding. Like you want justice for your two dead troopers and if you get that justice by catching the killers, you get that justice for the families of the dead men. I see a lot of murder vics on my job and that can wear on your mind at times, but you have to shake it off and move on.

Mason said, "I couldn't do that on a regular basis. I give you a lot of credit for doing what you do."

"Like I said, it's about getting justice for the victims and their families."

Mason pulled his car onto a small dirt trail and stopped the car. He said, "We'll have to walk into the place where the first murder happened. It's not too far." Both men got out of the car and started down a small pathway that was lined with trees on both sides. Sean touched the glock pistol on his side as he looked at the thick woods around him.

After a short walk Mason stopped on the pathway and pointed to a tree and said, "This is where the first victim was strung up. He wasn't pulled up too high on the tree, but still, whoever pulled him up had to be somewhat strong to even pull him up a little."

Sean asked Mason, "So no prints or DNA from the rope?"

"No, nothing was left at the scene. There was a lot of blood, mainly from when the vic's dick was cut off and from the skin removed from the vic's face."

"The guy who was shot at on his atv, didn't see who shot at him?" Sean asked.

"No he didn't see shit. He got out of here as fast as he could. He knew he was being shot at by a rifle from the sound the gun made," Mason answered.

"Well, I'm sure your techs processed all that was here. Can we head to the next crime scene?" Sean asked as he wrote down a few things on a note pad.

"Yes we can and it really isn't that far away. My troopers were checking out all the camps in the area and the one where they were killed is down the road and we can drive down to it. Both men walked back to the car. Mason backed the car out onto North Road and drove a short distance down the road and soon pulled into a driveway that led to a camp. The men got out of the car and Sean said, "I know this is hard for you to revisit where your men were killed, but we want justice for them."

"I want justice for them too and so let's view the back of the camp where they were killed."

"What about inside the camp first?" Sean asked.

"Sure, if that's what you want."

The men walked into the camp, as Mason had a key to the door, which he got from relatives of the man who was killed at the scene along with his two troopers.

Sean looked around at the kitchen and then walked into the bedroom and glanced at the bed. He turned to face the captain and asked, "What happened to the blankets and sheets from the bed?"

"There was nothing on the bed. That's the way we found it."

"So your techs didn't remove them?"

"No, like I said there were no blankets or sheets on the bed."

Sean made another note in his small book and followed Mason to the back of the camp. Mason pointed to a tree and said, "That's where the camp owner was found nailed to the tree, with his penis stuffed in his mouth and again, lots of blood around the tree. My two troopers had been pulled under the tree after shots to both their backs and heads."

"That's the part that makes me think that there had to be two people involved in killing your troopers. If they checked the inside of the camp first and found no one inside, then how in hell did they get shot from behind? You say they were pulled under the tree also?"

"That's right because we did see some drag marks, but it looked as though most of the drag marks were cleared away."

Sean again wrote in his note pad as he looked over the scene. He then asked, "The only prints found here were from the camp owner. No DNA in or out of the house or others?"

"We compared relatives of the dead camp owner with prints found with their prints and all prints were from the relatives or from the owner. Relatives were all accounted for on the day of the killings."

"Well, I still think this scene looks like it could have been a plan to ambush your troopers. Probably, that's why the camp owner was attached to the tree. The troopers could have had their focus on the vic and been shot from behind. It's just not clear right now."

"I agree with you. They were taken by surprise and paid the ultimate price for it. Are you ready to go to the motel crime scene?"

"Yes, we can go." Sean said and then turned and said to the spot where the troopers were killed, "We'll get the bastards for you."

When both men were in the car, Mason said, "Now at this motel we have to play it cool because I don't want any one from the motel contacting my boss and questioning why I am at the motel again, after the case has been closed. We need an excuse as to why we are there."

"I understand what you mean. What do you have in mind?"

"The reward has been paid to the maid and to the owner of the motel and they don't want to lose it by us snooping around and finding something that will cause that to happen."

"Let me play it by ear and you stay in the car out of sight," Sean said.

"What do you plan to do in order to see the room where the guy killed himself?"

"Just get us there and let me think on the way," Sean replied.

When they arrived at the motel, Mason pulled around to the back of the place and Sean got out of the car and walked into the office out front. He said to the person at the check-in counter, "Hello there, I'm W. B. Fields from the State Health Department and I need to do a quick check on the room where a person recently killed himself. It is just a check to see that air quality is ok after repairs were made. It will only take a few minutes. Basically just have to have a quick look at the room. Can you direct me to the room?"

The young man behind the counter said, "The owner isn't here right now. Do I need to contact him first?"

"Oh hell no. This is just a routine thing to cover your ass on insurance. It will only take a few minutes. I do this all the time."

Sean was led to the room he wanted to see and the man opened the door. Sean walked inside and the man followed him in. Sean looked around and pretended to breathe in deeply. He then said to the man, "Smells ok with no paint odor." Sean walked to where the bed was and looked at the wall with plaster in a hole that was covered with fresh paint. The hole was straight back in the wall, alined with the middle of the bed. Sean asked the man, "Is the bed in the same location it was when the guy killed himself?"

The man answered, "What does that have to do with air smells?"

"Well you see, plaster can make air smell odd if it isn't done correctly. There is plaster on the wall behind the bed. So the bed is in the same place right?"

The man said, "Yes, it is. All our beds are like this one."

Sean looked under the bed and saw the imprints on the carpet. It hadn't been moved. "That about does it. The room passed with flying colors. Now I have to go to my next stop down near Pittsburgh. I'll send you my report. Thanks for your help." Sean shook the man's hand and walked out the door and quickly to the car where Mason was waiting. Mason then quickly drove away without being seen.

"That was fun," Sean said with a smile.

As Mason drove, he asked, "What did you see in that room and how did you get inside?"

"I was W. B. Fields, State Health Department, checking on air quality of the room, after the death in the room. Got to have clean air you know. Mason laughed and Sean continued, "Anyway the bed was in the same location as it was when the man was killed and the room had been painted. The plaster on the wall filled a hole which was neither left nor right, but straight back from the middle of the bed, which is a tell that perhaps someone else pulled the trigger and then placed the gun in the hand of the man. Again, I was in a hurry to get in and out of there as fast as I could. I saw what I needed to anyway."

"Well, nice name you picked for yourself."

"I thought it worked well too," Sean said smiling.

"What's next?" Mason asked.

"I need a beer for sure," came the answer from Sean.

"Wise plan. Where to?"

"Since we are trying to stay out of the public's eyes and out of your supervisor's knowledge of our on the sly investigation, we can rehash today at my friend's house and I know he has Harp beer at his house."

"What exactly is Harp beer?" Mason asked.

"It is Irish beer. Tastes great and is 5% alcohol content, so you know you are drinking beer. Plus it is brewed in Ireland."

"Sounds like it is Harp time," Mason said.

Sean smiled as he made some more notes in his notebook.

Penny Sullivan was talking with Melissa Travers about the fire at the cabin that injured several firemen. "So the fire inspector claimed that the explosion was caused by a probable leak in one of the propane tanks inside the cabin. But what I don't understand is what set the tank on fire even if it was leaking?"

"I don't understand the whole propane tank theory myself. According to firemen who I talked with, propane tanks can cause large explosions, but there are safety measures on the tanks in case a leak happens. However, knowledge of propane tanks is something I'm not aware of and I'll be the first to admit it," Melissa said.

"I'm not knowledgeable about propane tanks either, but I'm going to do some research on the subject as soon as I get home," Penny added.

Willy and Kite were once again in a small motel outside of Marshton and Willy said, "That investigator who was involved at the farm where my brother was killed is from Pittsburgh from what I read in those papers written at the time of the shoot-out at the farm. So what I was thinking was to either finish up here and then pay a visit to that Roon guy and his wife in Pittsburgh. She was at the scene with that Roon investigator too. She is a doctor of some type. She'll need more than a doctor when I'm done with her."

"What else do we have to do in this fucked up place?" Kite asked.

"That fucking newspaper in Marshton wrote some bad shit about my brother and his friends and I want to make the assholes pay for what they wrote. I've been thinking about blowing the paper's office and printing machines into dust. I'm getting good at making bombs,"

Willy said.

Kite replied, "We will be lucky if you don't blow our asses up. Why can't we just get out now?"

"I want to get all the revenge that I can while we are here. Besides don't you like the thrill of killing out here in nature?"

"Fuck you Willy and nature too!"

"Let's get something to eat. What do you want to eat?"

"You mean after you eat me?"

Willy laughed and got on the bed with Kite.

Sean and Mason sat around the patio table at Alex's house and each man had a bottle of Harp beer in front of them. They were talking about what Sean observed at the crime scenes that they visited today.

"Mainly, I strongly believe that two killers have been involved and that one of them is probably a woman. I also believe that the guy at the motel did not, I repeat, did not off himself due to the shot going straight back from the bed and I still could see the bullet hole that had been plastered over. Also it would take a strong person to have hanged a guy from a tree and the dead guy in the motel, you told me was very small and not the strong type judging from his body weight. Where your troopers were ambushed also points to an ambush where two killers were involved and as I said, one was a woman who could have set the troopers up to be ambushed. That is just a hunch on my part mind you," Sean said as he took a long drink from his beer.

"Sean, I do agree with what you have said. I think we need to meet with Chief Smithson tomorrow and have access to his computer. That way we can quickly check on information which we might need. If we are going to find these killers we need to find out what their motive is."

"Maybe they are just fucking insane or druggies, totally out of it?" Sean said.

"Ok, I'll call the chief and call you back with a time that we can meet. Thanks again for all of your help Sean. See you tomorrow."

Mason shook hands with Sean and left.

Jesse walked out to the patio and asked, "So Sean, are you done work for today?"

"Yes, I am. What about you? Are you getting the information you need for your case?"

Jesse sat down at the patio table. She sat a glass on wine on the table and said, "I'm getting the information ok but it's not like I can look into our client's eyes while getting the information. That means a lot to me. Right now I am just getting the details from my partner, who is also involved in the case. I'm just not used to not talking face to face with a client."

"I agree that it must be difficult for you. I wouldn't want to base an interview of a possible suspect from just my partner's opinions sent to me on a fax machine, even if I have trust in my partner. Can you handle it, not being there?"

"I'm trying, but it isn't easy, to say the least."

"Do you want to fly back to the city to prepare for the case?"

"No, not yet, but I might have to, depending on how long you plan to remain here. How much longer are you going to stay here?"

"Not much longer. There is only so much I can do to help get them on track to find the real killers. Right now there is no real motive or tie-ins to the killings that took place."

"One thing in my cases, which I always do, no matter what the client has told me, is to look into the past, to make sure I'm getting a clear understanding of basically, what is what," Jesse said.

Sean thought for a moment, took a sip of his beer and got up and kissed his wife.

"What was that for?" Jesse said surprised.

Sean kissed her again and said, "Just that you are so smart, pretty and I am so glad I am married to you."

Later the evening Jesse, Sean, Alex and Jeanene were at a table in Abelli's. The place was crowded and Alex walked to the bar to order drinks. Courtney Collins was tending bar and said, "Hello Alex, what can I get for you?"

Alex ordered two Harps, a vodka sunrise and a glass of red wine. Sean got up and helped Alex carry the drinks back to the table. Alex sat down and said, "Here's hoping you two had successful afternoons."

Alex then raised his bottle to toast his friends.

Sean said, "And here's to Alex for being both a friend and host to us." Sean raised his bottle to retoast Alex.

Jeanene asked Jesse, "Are you able to work your case from here without much trouble?"

"I wouldn't exactly say that it is what I am used to, but so far it is ok," Jesse answered and smiled at Sean.

Laurie, came to the table and took the food orders and said, "Thanks for getting the drinks for me. It is really busy tonight and I'm the only waitress on tonight."

All four at the table ordered the special, which was either tacos el Deano or Salmon Val style. The tacos had a meaty sauce with a secret recipe and the salmon had a lemon sauce also from a secret recipe.

After dinner, Sean said, "Since we walked down here through the park, let's show Jesse and Jeanene the very old and cool bar where we watched football. What do you say?" No one answered Sean, so he said, "I'll pay the bill and see you all outside."

It was a short walk from Abelli's to The Marsh bar and as they walked Sean said the the two women, "This bar could be located back in time and would fit right in the Revolutionary War days, with people making a plan for the Boston Tea Party or out west in a frontier town with Billy the Kid at the bar having a beer or two."

Jesse said, "I take it you relate to the place Sean?"

"Yes I do. Our rugby team would have loved this place, right Alex?"

"You got it Sean," Alex said.

When the four of them walked into the bar, there was an open table near the pool table. Everyone at the bar glanced at them as they sat at the table. Cody Wayne, the owner was at his usual seat at the end of the bar and gave Alex a nod. Laura, was tending bar and Alex walked to the bar and ordered three Bud Lights and a cherry wine cooler. Cody Wayne said to Alex, "Where did you find the pretty ladies?"

Alex pointed to Jesse and said, "That's Sean's wife Jesse and the other lady is Jeanene, who teaches with me. You know Sean from our football day in here."

Jesse took a sip of her beer and said, "This place is vintage. You are right Sean, it could fit back in time."

"It has history written all around the walls," Jeanene said.

Alex said, "Look over past the pool table. There is an old jukebox that still works. Go look at it."

Jesse and Jeanene walked over to the jukebox and were reading the songs listed inside. When the came back to the table, Jeanene said, "Wow, there are some really old songs on there."

"Can we play some songs?" Jesse asked Alex.

"Cody, can we play a few songs?" Alex asked.

"Sure, go ahead."

"How much does it cost?" Jesse asked.

"It's free. Just push the buttons," Cody said with a smile.

Jesse and Jeanene walked to the jukebox and were laughing. Soon an old Elvis song started playing. Alex looked at Sean saying, "Takes you back in time doesn't it?"

The next song started playing and Sean stood up and raised his arms. The song was from 1975, by a band called Hello. The song was, "Back In the New York Groove." Sean started to do a little dance by the pool table and Jim Sparta and Art Fisher at the bar turned to watch Sean.

Jesse joined Sean dancing. When the song ended Sean kissed his wife for playing the song. Sean ordered another round of drinks and bought Cody, Sparta and Fisher drinks also. He then sat next to Cody and asked him in a quiet voice, "What the hell happened here in the recent past that people got hurt or killed?"

"You must mean that shoot-out at a farm where people were killing and eating people they killed. The local folks put an end to that in a shoot-out. That was awhile back."

"They were actually eating the people they killed?"

"Yeah, can you believe it? Real, live cannibals here in Marshton?"

"Were the people from here?"

"No, some other place. I can't remember exactly where, but not from here." A song by Del Shannon was playing, Runaway.

"So people from here killed the killers?" Sean asked.

"Most of them. Some woman survived and is in prison somewhere and also a local guy who was the medical examiner. He was fucking the woman and he is in prison too."

"Well, that was quite the happening around here," Sean said.

"Yeah, that it was," Cody said and took a drink of his beer.

An hour later, Sean, Jesse, Jeanene and Alex were on their walk home through the park and Alex was relating to Sean what he remembered about the shoot-out at the farm and how it ended.

As the group stopped at the tennis courts to watch some people playing, Alex asked Sean, "So you think that the key to solving the whole thing going on is a revenge factor by some pissed off person or persons?"

"That I do and now we need to find out who, as you said, is the pissed off person seeking revenge for some reason," Sean stated.

Jesse picked up a tennis ball that was hit over the fence near where she was standing and tossed it back to the players on the court. The group began walking again on the way to Alex's house away from the lights near the tennis courts.

CHAPTER 17

What Is What

At Chief Smithson's office the next morning, Sean, Captain Mason and the Smithson were seated around a table. Sean asked, "Now this may not be on the right track in this investigation but perhaps it can put us on the right track. Who all was involved in that shoot-out at that farm where those criminals were selling body organs and eating some victims?"

"What in hell does that have to do with the killers we are looking for?" the chief asked puzzled.

"Well, it just might have everything to do with the killers we are looking for," Sean replied.

"I don't get where you are heading Sean," Mason said.

"First of all just tell me what local people were involved in bringing down those killers back at that farm," Sean said.

The chief looked over at Captain Mason and then said, "As I recall, there were quite a few. Ok, here's the list of people:

Denny James
Mouse James
Tracy James
Brian James
Roberto Browning
Mike Mayer
Patty Mayer
Chip Cline
Dave Roon
Linda Ortman

Penny Sullivan anyone who I forgot, Captain?"

"You are much more aware of who was involved back then, than I am," Mason answered.

"I think that is every one, that I can remember. Now why do you want to know who was involved Sean?" the chief asked.

"Now tell me who has been involved in an accident, a strange occurance, a crime, or anything that was reported to you recently, no matter how far out it may seem," Sean said.

The chief looked at Sean and said, "This seems far out to me Sean. Where are you going with this?"

"Just trust me on this. Can you get the info from your computer? Just pull up the data from the point where that first murder happened in the woods. Can you do that chief?"

"I can do it but it might take some time. Why don't you two have another cup of coffee," the chief said as he got up and went over to his computer.

After twenty minutes the chief returned to the table with a stack of printouts. "Here you go Sean," the chief said as he tossed the sheets on the table.

"Now chief I need you to scan the reports and list the people who were involved in that fire fight back in time and list what they were involved with in any of these reports," Sean said.

"I'll do it but I still don't get what you are up to," the chief said.

"Ok, here's what I got from the reports:

Mike Mayer was bitten by a rattlesnake and was hospitalized.

Tracy James was injured in a hit and run. Still unsolved.

Mouse James had his truck catch fire at the fire hall.

Roberto Browing died of an OD. that's anyone who was at the shoot-out from the reports."

"Now, who has not been in town recently, from the first list you gave me?" Sean asked.

"Let's see, Denny James is on a safari in Africa. Brain James is in California for some show he is involved in. Roon and Ortman are now married and live in Pittsburgh."

"So, Patty Mayer, Chip Cline and Penny Sullivan are still in town, right?" Sean asked.

"That's right and they haven't been in any reported happenings, except Patty took her husband to the hospital following the snake bite. Chip Cline was out of town for a meeting at the recent camp explosion and Penny Sullivan runs the local paper."

"Well, do you see what I'm getting at now?" Sean said as he looked at both other men seated at the table.

Mason looked at Sean and said, "You are trying to paint a picture of a revenge factor. Isn't that right Sean?"

"You are correct. I am leaning in that direction, because it would be one hell of a motive and give us a direction to go in," Sean said looking at Smithson and Mason.

"You mean you think that a person is seeking revenge on those involved back when that fire fight took place?" the chief asked Sean.

"I think it is something we have to consider, judging from those who have been involved in police reports recently," Sean replied to the chief.

"I agree with Sean. It gives a new direction to consider," Captain Mason said.

"We need to find out who is related to those who were killed during that fire fight. It would tie-in the revenge factor,"Sean stated.

"That can be a problem because the FBI down loaded the files from our computers and they have the data we will need. If this investigation didn't have to be on the sly, I might be able to get the information we need," Mason said.

"Why in hell did they do that?" Sean asked.

"Who knows why the FBI does anything? I think they were pissed that locals solved the whole thing and not them. They probably did it to cover their own asses. Anyway, they did it," Mason said in a pissed off tone.

"I'll see what I can find out without letting the fact out that we are doing our own investigation. Let me get to it later today," the chief related.

"You know if we are right about the revenge factor, and I think we are, then other people involved in that fire fight could be in danger. What do we do about that?" Sean said.

"That's a good question right now. How do we warn them without letting on what we are up to?" Mason asked.

"I don't have an answer to that," the chief stated.

"Shit, see what you can find out later on who might be a relative of those killed in the shoot-out. What about the two who survived. They are in prison aren't they? They might know the info we need in terms of relatives of those who were killed?" Sean asked.

"Again, how do we contact them without letting on that we are doing our own investigation?" Mason asked.

"Shit again, I guess we can't without putting you in trouble with your head man," Sean said looking at Mason.

"This is really fucked up. Here we have a direction to go in and we have to cover our ass every step of the way. Nice way to solve the mystery of who killed my troopers and others," Mason said.

"Well we have to play with the hand that has been dealt to us, thanks to your boss at regional headquarters for rushing to close the case, just to make him look good," Chief Smithson said.

"What do you plan to do chief?" Mason asked.

"I have a friend who might be able to get us the information we need. He is a computer expert named Carl Clapton and I need to talk to him to see if he can help us on this. He has helped me in the past. I'll get ahold of him today," The chief said. The meeting ended and Sean and Mason walked out of the police station.

"I just hope the chief can get us the information we need to move ahead in our investigation and get it without letting on what we are up to," Mason said.

"I'll be talking to you later after you are contacted by the chief. So long," Sean said as he walked to his rented car.

After Sean and Captain Mason left his office, Smithson placed a call to Carl Clapton. "Hello Carl, this is Norm Smithson, I was wondering if you can stop by the station today. I need your help on a problem I am working on?"

"Yes, I can stop down in about an hour. Can you give me a clue on what the problem is?"

"It involves computers and that's why I'm on the phone with you. I need you to seek out some information for me," the chief answered.

"Is the problem police business?" Carl asked.

"Well, yes and no. We will go over that when you stop by the station."

"Sounds most interesting. I'll see you soon."

The chief sat at his desk and wondered just how he was going to ask Carl to do some hacking into files that the FBI had down loaded from Mason's computers. He got up from his desk and walked out back of the station to smoke a Marlboro and think. As the chief sat at a small picnic table and smoked, he thought of the fire at JK's Tavern and then the recent fire at the cabin in the woods. "Damn," he said out loud and put out his Marlboro and walked back inside the station and into his office. He sat at his desk and made some notes about the two fires he had just thought about while smoking outside. He thought to himself that the revenge issue now makes more and more sense. Sean was exactly right.

In the small motel room Willy said to Kite, "We have been lucky driving around in all of these ripped off cars. That is getting to be a problem."

"So what do you plan to do about it?" Kite asked.

"Here's what I've been thinking about, we can either take a bus to Buffalo and hit the casino up there and find us a victim who is single and has a car we can get from him after we off him, or we can take a chance on driving the last car we got that is no doubt hot and the police are looking for it. What do you think?"

"Holy shit, you mean you actually want my advice?"

"Yes, you are part of this adventure too."

"If you are set on doing anymore shit around here, then we need a car that the cops aren't looking for and to get one in another state would probably be smart. That's what I think."

Willy thought a few seconds and said, "Ok, we will head to Buffalo and get us a car that won't be hot, at least for a time period. Then we come back here and do one more major job."

"What the hell is one more major job?" Kite asked and then said, "I'm sure you don't mean a blow job, so what are you talking about?"

"I'll tell you on the ride to Buffalo. We'll take a chance and drive to Buffalo, but we'll take the back roads up there."

Chief Smithson was talking to Carl Clapton in his office and he said to Clapton, "So we need the information that the FBI down loaded and then erased from the state police computers."

Clapton asked, "Why did the FBI do that? That was a prick move on their part."

"Captain Mason is pissed about it, since we need the names of any relatives alive that were related to those two nuts that were killed in that shoot-out back at the farm across the border. Remember that the FBI was working the case and they must not have been too happy that the group of locals solved the case by killing two of the killers and catching the other two people who were at the farm. Those two alive are in prison. We need names of the relatives of the two dead guys so we can figure out if there are killers still out there, and probably are the ones who killed Mason's men recently. Now Carl, you know what I am telling you has to stay between us. You can't tell any body. Is that clear?"

"I understand and I'll keep my mouth shut about what you are doing. In order to hack into FBI files will require me contacting some friends of mine who are involved in the spectre net."

Smithson looked confused and asked, "What exactly is the spectre net?"

"Spectre is french for *ghost* and that's what the spectre net is all about. You know, keeping activities invisible. Some of the very best hackers are involved in the spectre net. The FBI, with all of their computer geeks haven't a clue how to penetrate the spectre net. I will need the name of the file first of all. What will happen, I think, will be that it will be a very quick strike into the file, that will look like a computer glitch. In and out with the info you need. Like a key word in the file . . . like the word relatives . . . or a couple of words brothers or sisters. See, in and out and the feds have no clue what happened and cannot trace anything. So, I need you to get me the file name that the feds took from Mason's computer."

"I'll call Mason on his phone right now. Give me a minute."

Chief Smithson placed a call to Captain Mason on his private phone and after talking with him for less than a minute, he ended the call and looked at his friend Carl Clapton.

Clapton asked, "What did you find out?"

"The name of the file is: 292-PN," Smithson answered.

"I will see what can be done. You also know to keep me far away from what you guys are trying to do. I hope I can help you find who you are looking for out there. I'll contact you if and when I get the info you are looking for."

The chief stood up and walked Clapton to the door. He shook Clapton's hand and said, "Thanks a million for helping me out on this Carl."

"Remember, I'm a ghost on this whole thing."

"You are invisible as far as I'm concerned. What about that ghost net? Is it really protected so the feds can't tell what's happening?"

Clapton smiled and said, "Algorithms and magnetic pulses that I helped design provide the ghost staying a ghost." Carl then walked down the steps. The chief walked back inside his office and placed another call to Captain Mason. He told Mason that Clapton was going to try to get the information they needed and would call again, once he heard back from Clapton. Mason thanked him for getting his friend, Carl Clapton involved.

Smithson ended the call by saying, "As far as any person knows, he has never been involved."

"I get it," Mason said.

Sean and Jesse were talking in the kitchen of Alex's house. It had just started to rain outside and Jesse pointed at the sky where a rainbow appeared, as the sun and rain came together. Jesse said, "You sure never get to see many rainbows in the city. That is beautiful."

"I agree. It makes you realize how much of nature we miss by living in the city. Speaking of the city, what did the law office say about you returning in order to meet the client face to face?"

"They want me to fly back to get a meeting set. There's really not much I can do about it. I'll have to go back in the next day or two and it will take me a couple of days there to get things squared away with my partner, who will be on the case with me. I'll miss you."

"I'll miss you too. I don't know how much longer I'll be here. Things may be breaking in this investigation if we can get the information we need. It's been like trying to investigate with one hand tied behind your back and the other one over one eye. It sucks."

"Let's take a walk in the rain. It's not raining that hard and there is no lightning. It will feel good," Jesse said.

Sean got up and kissed Jesse and they walked outside into the light rain.

Chief Smithson got a text from Carl Clapton and he was completely surprised at how quick the information he wanted was gotten by his computer friend. It took less than an hour. The text read, "The name of the man known as Tat, who was killed back when the fire fight at the farm in Greenstone, New York, happened to have a name on file: Charles Whiteside and he had a younger brother named William Whiteside. Their parents died in a crash and the boys were placed in separate foster homes. When Charles was sixteen, he ran away from the foster home. The foster parents of William, who was fourteen, were found murdered and William vanished. The state this happened in was California. There was nothing else in file 292-PN. The text from Carl stated that most of the file had been deleted." The text ended with, "I hope this helps."

Smithson went to his office computer and typed in the names from the text he had just got from Carl Clapton. He found that Charles Whiteside had served time for tax evasion. There was nothing on William Whiteside. So the only clues to help in the investigation were the two Whiteside names and thanks to the damn FBI, the majority of file 292-PN had been erased. "Not much to go on," the chief said to himself.

CHAPTER 18

A Coming Together

A day later Sean drove Jesse to the Marshton airport, where her law firm's corporate plane picked her up and Sean watched the plane vanish into the clouds and he wondered just how much longer he would be in Marshton in an attempt to bring the investigation to an end.

On the ride to Buffalo on the back roads, Willy told Kite that he wanted to leave Marshton by causing something that they wouldn't soon forget and that was by blowing the Marshton Paper's office and printing machines all to hell. It would take some time to plan it out and get the materials to make several bombs and that could be done while they were in Buffalo. Kite told Willy that he'd probably blow them up while he was making the bombs. Willy just laughed and continued to drive on the small back roads in the direction of Buffalo.

An hour after Sean got to Alex's house his phone rang. It was Mark Mason who said, "I spoke to Chief Smithson and he heard back from his computer friend." Mason then related to Sean what the chief had told him. "The chief said that we could meet in his office in an hour to talk over what was in the state police file. The chief said that most of the file was erased, but there were a couple of names in the file that may help us."

Sean agreed to be at the chief's office in an hour and ended the call.

He then wrote a note for Alex to read, telling him that he would be at Chief Smithson's office and that Jesse was on her way to New York City. Alex was teaching a morning class at the college. Sean had a cup of coffee in his hand and walked to look at a big framed photo of the rugby team he and Alex played on in the city. Sean smiled when he thought back to a time the rugby team was celebrating a victory at the bar, called Mac's, and was owned by Jeff and Julia. Jeff was on the rugby team; and he always hosted the team after their games. The weekend was the Memorial Day weekend and Alex always played the song that was a tribute to the ship the Reuben James, because his father and uncle had a relative on the ship that was sunk by a U-boat off the Iceland coast in late October, 1941. Johnny Horton sang his favorite version of the song, but the song was written by Woody Guthrie. A guy at the bar made the mistake by saying, "Who is playing this shit? It sucks!"

Alex walked over to the guy and smiled. He ordered a glass of beer from Julia, who was tending bar. She knew something was not right because Alex always drank Harp beer. Alex then faced the man who said the stuff about the song. Sean got a grin on his face as he recalled what Alex did next. Alex looked at the man and said, "The song is about 100 dead sailors who were lost on the Reuben James, you asshole." Alex then tossed a full glass of beer in the man's face. The man was shocked and just stood there, not daring to start a fight with a room full of rugby players. Jeff, the owner of the bar said to the man who had beer dripping from his face, "Man over board." Sean raised his coffee cup in a toast to his former rugby team, his friend Alex and the Reuben James.

Willy stopped at several hardware stores and bought several pieces of pipe and sealing caps. He then stopped at a fireworks store and bought several large sky rockets. Then he drove to a store that sold guns and ammo and he bought a box of shotgun shells. At each stop Kite sat in the car and wondered just what Willy was planning to do with the materials he was buying. She was wishing she was high and as she sat there she thought about getting away from Willy, but he kept her high when she wanted to be, which was most of her waking hours and he was good in bed. Plus, she thought, she had no where to go without him right now. She also knew that she could end up in jail or dead staying with him.

When Sean arrived at the police station the chief and Captain Mason were in the chief's office. "Welcome aboard. Have a chair," the chief said to Sean. "We were just going over the little that the file had left in it."

Sean sat down and asked, "Not much help then?"

"We have two names, Charles and William Whiteside. Charles was the dead guy at the fire fight in Greenstone and William vanished from a foster home, where the foster parents had been murdered. There seems to be no record of William after he vanished. If there ever were photos of him, they vanished along with him back at the age of fourteen," Mason added.

"What about photos from schools or child service agencies?" Sean asked.

"The feds probably had them, but no doubt they vanished into the Devil's Triangle along with other information that the file contained, which could have helped us," the chief stated.

"Again, why did they do it? You know delete the file and take the info from the state police computers?" Sean asked.

"My guess is simply to cover their own asses for fucking up the investigation in the first place back when that case ended in Greenstone," Mason said, "and we can't just go and ask them why they did it can we?"

"No, and even if we could, they wouldn't give us a straight answer to why they did it. It would probably be the routine answer of "Classified," the chief said with a smile.

"I have to be back at headquarters soon, as the vacation I took is over after this weekend ends and we have not much to show for it, other than we know that the motel room scene was a set-up and those who killed my troopers are still at large," Mason said in a loud voice.

"Are any of your officers checking out motels in the area or reports of stolen cars in the area chief?" Sean asked.

"Yes, they are on it. Nothing that has helped so far," the chief answered.

"Have they been asking if a man and woman checked-in to a room and were from out of the area, or acted strange?" Sean asked.

"Shit, Sean, a massive amount of men and women check into motels all the time. Either just traveling or wanting to get laid, or for who knows why. That could take us no where," the chief replied.

"Then it seems our hands are tied at this point," Sean said.

"At least I can check out the part about stolen cars when I am back on duty at headquarters. I'll have access to my computers and it won't look like I'm involved in my own investigation," Mason said.

"I don't know how much longer I can remain in the area. My captain from the city is friends with your Miss Clarkson and he is doing her a favor by letting me help out with the investigation. However, he could want me back at anytime, if we can't come up with some positive directions in order to find the real killers," Sean said.

"By the way, about that recent fire at the cabin in the woods, you know the fire chief was out of town when the fire happened and the acting chief was in charge. He was injured critically. The fire chief, who was out of town, was Chip Cline, who was involved in the fire fight at the farm in Greenstone. I mean that leads to the revenge factor and also the fire at JK's tavern, is where a lot of the other people involved in that fire fight used to hang out. So again, it ties into the revenge factor.

It sure makes your point about revenge being the cause of the killings and other happenings around here," the chief said.

"I'd say you are right about that Norm," Mason stated.

"Like we spoke about before, do we put out a warning to the people involved in that fight at the farm?" Sean asked.

"I could talk to each of them and say that I'm investigating on my own and keep the state police involvement out of it. How does that sound to you two?" Smithson said waiting for an answer.

"I think that's a great idea. We have to warn them," Sean said.

"I agree with Sean. Go ahead and talk to those people who were involved," Mason replied.

"Then, where do we go from after I give out the warning?" the chief asked.

"Give the warning and we can meet later or tomorrow," Mason said.

At a cheap motel in Buffalo, New York, Willy laid the materials he had bought on the bed: a hacksaw to cut the pipes sealing caps

- a box of 12 gauge shells
- several different fireworks
- a small drill
- and a few small tools

"Ok Kite my dear, while I work on these bombs, you can go to the laundro mat we saw down the street and wash our clothes, because they need it."

"Are you sure you know what you are doing making these bombs?"

"I know what I'm doing."

"I'll walk down to wash the clothes and I hope the motel is still here when I get back," Kite said with a slight laugh.

Later that day, after Alex returned from teaching his class, he took Sean to a small bar called Paul's Place. When they got there Alex spoke to the owner, Paul and then took two beers out to the patio and sat down with Sean. A few minutes later Paul walked out and sat down with Alex and Sean. He handed Alex and Sean each a cigar. "Thanks for the Cubans Paul. I can always count on you," Alex said.

"Yes, but remember our policy, "don't ask and don't tell," Paul said with a smile. Both Alex and Sean understood what Paul meant because Cuban cigars were still illegal in this country.

"Damn, these are great cigars," Alex said as he inhaled deeply. As the men were smoking, Sean's phone rang. Sean stood and walked to the far end of the patio.

"Hello Jesse. How was your flight back to the city?"

"It was a smooth flight and the limo ride to the firm was a nice change from taxis. How are things on your end?"

"Not much has changed. We are quite certain that revenge is involved in the killings."

"You make sure you are careful up there."

"I will and I hope I'll be back in your arms soon."

"I will call you tomorrow. Love you a lot."

"Love you as much if not more." The call ended and Sean walked back to the patio table and took a puff on his cigar, thinking how much he loved his wife.

"So, I take it that was Jesse. I can tell by that smile on your face," Alex said.

"She is back in the city and back working at her firm," Sean answered.

Alex told Paul that Jesse was Sean's wife and was a lawyer in New York City. He also told Paul that Sean was a detective in the city.

Paul raised his beer to toast Sean and the men talked of crime in New York and why Sean was here in Marshton.

When Kite returned from washing their clothes Willy was still working on his pipe bombs. He had five bombs made and laid out on the bed. "Only one more to go and I'll be done. Want to see how I make them?" Willy asked.

"I don't want anything to do with any bomb," Kite said.

"Well I'll tell you what I do. First cut the pipes to the length I want.

Next I put a cap on one end of the pipe. Then I fill the pipe with gun powder or black powder from the fireworks. Then put in the pellets from the shells. Then drill a small hole in the other cap and put the fuse into the pipe and finally seal around where the fuse went in. That's all there is to it until I use them."

"Like I said, bombs are your thing, not mine. So how are we going to get a different car and get out of here?"

"I am almost out of the plates we got in Ohio, so I can't keep switching plates around on the cars we steal. We need to get a car to get us back to Marshton. However, if we drive at night we can go to that casino in that town of Salamanca and check cars in that dark parking lot for keys that people attach with a magnet under the area by their wheels. They do it in case they lose a key or lock it accidently in their car. A lot of people do that now."

"So we just feel under where you said to look?"

"Right and then we leave the car we have now and off we go to do the final thing I have planned for that town of Marshton."

"Let me ask you, are those damn bombs safe to keep in this room?"

"Perfectly safe. Now lets walk out to a bar and have some fun," Willy said.

CHAPTER 19

Still At Large

Chief Smithson made a list with phone numbers and addresses of all of those involved in the fight at the farm in Greenstone. He began to call each name on the list. He knew all the people on the list, even though he wasn't the chief of police back when the fight at the farm happened. He told each person he contacted on the list that the people or person responsible for the recent killings could still be around the area and that the case should not have been closed by the head of the state police. He also told them to be very careful until further notice and to keep this information out of public knowledge for the time being as he did not want the fact that he was conducting an investigation on his own to get back to the head of the state police. The people he had contacted were shocked and not happy about the case being closed when the killer or killers could still be in the Marshton area.

At The Marsh bar later in the day, Jim Sparta and his brother, Rich Sparta were talking at a table. Jim asked his brother, "So who are you dating these days?"

"Well, I have a new woman that you haven't seen yet," Rich answered with a smile.

"You seem to always have a new woman. You do get around my brother," Jim said.

At that point, Tracy James and his wife Lisa walked into the bar and sat down with Jim and Rich Sparta. Judy, who was bartending, brought a round of drinks to the table. Tracy, who had a cast on his arm from the hit and run accident that he and his wife were recently involved in said, "I got a call from Chief Smithson today and he told us to be careful because the killer or killers could still be in the area. Do you believe that shit?"

Jim Sparta said, "I thought that the case was closed and the guy who did the killings was dead."

"Yeah, that's what we thought. But the chief said that the case was closed by the head of the state police too early and that we still need to be careful," Lisa stated.

"How the hell can that be? I mean didn't they have proof that the guy in the motel room did the killings?" Rich Sparta asked.

"I know what you are saying. We thought that it was all over too, but the chief warned us to be careful, because he thinks some friend or relative of a guy who was killed in that fight back at that farm in Greenstone, might be seeking revenge on any one who was involved in bringing down those assholes at the farm. Remember, I was involved in that fight with a lot of other local people," Tracy James said.

"So someone might be out there seeking revenge on local people?" Jim Sparta asked.

"It just might be true. The chief wasn't certain, but told us to be careful for the time being," Lisa said.

Phil, who was seated at the bar and talking to Judy turned to face the table and asked Tracy, "So what do you plan to do about what the chief related to you?"

"Keep a damn loaded gun on me at all times. What the hell else can I do?" Tracy replied.

"That was nice of the head of the state police to close the case before they were sure they had the right killer," Phil said.

"Yeah, that dirty bastard who closed the case doesn't have to live around here. So what the hell does he give a shit about us for?" Tracy said.

"Just make sure you are careful," Judy said.

"Maybe the chief can catch the killer before he can do any more harm around here," Rich Sparta said.

"We can only hope so," Lisa said.

"The chief can only do so much without the state police or FBI helping him," Jim Sparta related.

"At least he is smart enough to know that the killers may still be out there and I thank him for giving Lisa and I a warning," Tracy said.

"So did the chief warn all the other people who were involved in the fight at that farm?" Rich Sparta asked.

"I would guess that he did, because he called us and then said that he had other calls to make," Tracy said.

Bruce Bannon and Wanita Wallace came into the bar from the back door of the bar and sat down at the bar. Judy waited on them and Lisa James said, "I'll pay for their beers." she got up from the table and gave a hug to both Wanita and Bruce. She then said, "Thank you both all that you did to help Tracy and me on the day when we were hit."

Wanita said, "I'm just glad we were on the same road that you were on that day when that person ran into you and forced you off the road."

"How are you healing Tracy?" Bruce asked.

"This cast limits what I can do. I'm off work until the cast comes off and I can use my arm in a normal way," Tracy answered.

"That cast sure puts a limit on your golf game," Rich Sparta said with a grin.

"I could still beat you with one arm," Tracy smiled back at his friend.

Kite and Willy walked back to their motel from the bar where they were drinking and both of them had an alcohol high, which was quite different from the drug induced high that they were used to having. When they got inside the room Kite said, "I am quite fucked up right now. I'm not used to boozing it as much as we did."

"Me too. Let's take a damn nap," Willy said as he laid on the bed, not bothering to take off his clothes. Kite did the same.

Sean got a call from Chief Smithson and the chief told him that he had warned all those who were involved in the fire fight in Greenstone and the killer or killers may still be in the area and to be very careful.

Sean asked,"How did they respond to the warning you gave them?"

"Most of the people I spoke to were shocked to find out that they could be in danger and were not happy that the case had been closed by the state police. I can't say that I blame them for being pissed about the situation."

Sean said, "I can't either. That state police regional commander who closed the case will have a lot to answer for if we can catch the bastards really responsible for the killings.

I know Captain Mason is totally pissed that the case was closed."

"It's too bad that Mark can't get his troopers involved in our investigation, but that would bring his commander down on him in a hurry. So where do you think we should go from here, now that I've given out the warning that we spoke about?"

"I'm not sure. It's tough with just you, me and Mason trying to bring an end to the investigation."

"So we just wait for something else to happen to some other person?

That is a dangerous situation for a lot of people, if revenge is the factor of the killers," Smithson stated.

"I agree with what you are saying, but what else can we do at this point in time?" Sean said.

"This is really a cluster fuck in every way," the chief said in a most pissed off tone.

"Yeah, it certainly is. Like I said before, I don't know how much longer my captain in the city will let me remain here as long as we are at a standstill in our investigation."

"Well, I'll inform Mason about the warning I issued and ask him what he thinks we should do. Talk to you later."

Kite and Willy woke up from their alcohol induced nap and were now in a pizza parlor eating. Kite asked Willy, "When are we going back to Marshton to do whatever it is you have planned?"

"Tonight, after it gets dark, so we can travel on back roads and not worry about road checks or being pulled over. We can use the same car we have been using," Willy said.

"So you are going to use the bombs you made?"

"I didn't make them just for the fuck of it. Yes, I plan to blow that paper's office and that Sullivan lady all to hell," Willy said with a smile.

"Can't we just go back to Ohio and continue dealing, like we did before we came to the fucked up woods around here?"

"Look, we got involved with Blackburn and his boyfriend in Ohio and had all that meth to sell, before Blackburn dumped the shit into that pond. It would take time to get that much meth again to deal. I want to finish the revenge in Marshton and then we can talk about going back to Ohio. You know my brother helped me escape from that foster home back in California when I was fourteen. We offed those asshole foster parents and lived underground for several years. My brother left and went to Ohio and then got caught up in some shit where he did a prison sentence. When he got out he and his friends bought that little farm and dealt drugs. He was killed by the assholes from Marshton and that is why I'm getting revenge on them. He got me out of that foster situation and I owe him for that. Let's get out of here. I've had enough pizza. I want to get high."

"Sounds good to me," Kite said as she stood up from the table. They then walked back to the motel room and did lines of coke.

Alex came back home from teaching a class in European History and sat on the patio with Sean. Each man held a Harp beer and were talking about the investigation Sean was involved with, that seemed to be going nowhere. "Ater all the shit that these killers have pulled, there hasn't been any fingerprints at any scene and if they are using stolen cars, they must be taking off the tracking devices from the cars."

"How in hell do they do that?" Alex asked.

"Some cars have sensors under the hood. Others have devices built into the dash and some have a unit that can be seen on the dash. They are either taking out the sensors, smashing the unit on the dash or somehow making it impossible to get a location on a stolen car. There have been several cars that have been stolen in the immediate area. It is quite easy to get your hands on a car because a lot of people put an extra key attached with a magnet under to wheel wells or behind a car's bumper."

"Maybe the killers have their own car for all we know," Alex added.

"Maybe they do for all I know," Sean stated.

"So how long do you think you'll be able to stay involved in the investigation?"

"I would say not for much longer. I'm going to call my captain later and see what he has to say about it." The men changed the subject to the Yankees playing in the World Series.

Kite and Willy once again paid cash and checked into a small motel in a town called Olean. It was near Marshton, just over the New York State border. The man behind the check-in counter was eating a sandwich and did not ask for a credit card and accepted the cash. Once inside the small room, Willy told Kite what he planned to do to the Marshton Paper's Office. Willy said, "Like I said before, I plan to end this revenge adventure with a huge bang. I want to blow the office and that Sullivan lady at the same time. I also might try for the mayor and chief of police too."

"How do you plan to get the mayor and the chief?" Kite asked.

"I'll lure them over to the paper's office and then tie the fuckers up along with that editor. Then attach bombs to each of them with a long fuse that will touch off the bombs. The long fuse will give us time to get the fuck away before the building goes bang. Nice plan huh?"

"As long as we get out before your bang," Kite said.

Alex called Jeanene and asked her if she wanted to have dinner at Abelli's with Sean and him. She declined the invitation because she had a lot of work to prepare for her class tomorrow. So Alex and Sean drove to Abelli's to have dinner. Once they were seated at a table Sean related the news he had just gotten from his captain. Sean had called his captain while Alex was in the shower. "Well it looks like I'll be heading back to the city in two more days. I spoke to my captain while you were getting ready and he said to take a couple of more days up here and wrap up what you could do to help with the investigation. He was going to call Isabelle Clarkson and inform her. So my friend you will be rid of me very soon."

"I'm going to miss your company. It has been like having a brother staying with me."

"Outside of dealing with the sly investigation, I've enjoyed my stay with you. You have a good deal here in the not so peaceful woods. Plus you have a very good woman. I like her. She is a lot of fun."

"Yes she is wonderful and I also like her very much."

"Any wedding plans in the near future my friend?"

"One never knows does one," Alex said with a wide smile and walked to the bar to order two more beers.

Both men had ordered steaks and fries. Courtney, who was tending bar, said to Alex, "If it wasn't for you, we would probably not have this Harp beer in stock. You do seem to like it."

Alex replied, "Well Courtney, it does have a great taste and I learned to like it a long time ago."

"To each their own Alex," Courtney said. Alex walked back to the table and sat a beer in front of his friend.

"After you leave, it will be just myself drinking Harp beer in here."

"You are lucky this place ordered it just for you," Sean said as he raised the bottle to his lips and took a long sip.

"So what's the latest with Jesse and her big case in the city?"

"The last I spoke to her, she said there was a possibility that the case may settle out of court. It seems the person accused of the crime wants to keep his public image and might be willing to pay big bucks to keep what he did out of the public's knowledge."

"It probably has to do with forceable sex. In other words rape," Alex said.

"On that note, let's eat," Alex said.

When Sean's captain in the city called Isabelle Clarkson he told her that Sean had helped with the private investigation into the killings in Marshton as much as possible and he would be returning to New York City in a few days. Clarkson was dejected that the real killers had not been caught. She told the captain that she still felt that her boss had closed the case just to make himself look good and that justice for the two murdered troopers had not yet been achieved. The captain agreed with her but he needed Sean back in the city and could not continue to hide the fact that he was helping with an investigation in another state.

Clarkson thanked the captain, who she was friends with, then ended the call.

CHAPTER 20

Bang . . . Bang . . . Bang

Alex left for his class at the college and Sean called his wife and told her that he would be returning to the city in another day. Jesse was very happy to hear that and would make arrangements to meet him at the airport. Sean then went out to the patio and have a second cup of coffee.

Willy and Kite drove into the town of Marshton and talked about the plan to destroy the Marshton Paper building and how to get the mayor and chief of police to come over to the building. As they entered the town of Marshton, Willy said, "Are you sure you know what to say to the lady in charge of the paper when you call her?"

"Yes, we have been over it many damn times. I call the editor and tell her that I have some information that something bad is going to happen in Marshton and that the mayor and chief of police need to come over to the paper's office. I tell them that I will come to the office in an hour to give the details of the information. Then we go on with the plan we talked about to blow the building."

"You just do what you just said and the plan will work. Now let's get something to eat before you make the call and then we end this adventure."

"Are you sure that those bombs of your's will work?"

"Don't you worry your pretty little ass of your's about the bombs working. They will do the job. You worry about doing your job on that phone."

"I want to get out of this deal alive, not be part of the explosions."

"We each will go in there will a gun in our hands. Those assholes in the building will be at our mercy. Now let's get some food before you call."

In the Marshton Paper's office, Penny Sullivan and Melissa Travers were going over details about the upcoming Fall Festival, which was going to take place in a few weeks. It was 10:00am and Sullivan and Travers were the only two people who were in the building. On a table, front of them were all of the ads that were going to be in the special edition of the Fall Festival paper. Penny Sullivan said, "We have more ads than last year and we still have a lot of time left to get more ads. This could be a banner edition for the paper.

"The festival will give the community a chance to relax, after all that has happened recently. Closing down traffic to Main Street, with all the stores decorating and having it seem like a big party will give everyone a chance for fun," Melissa stated.

"I couldn't agree more Melissa."

Willy and Kite finished eating at Tracey's Restaurant and when they got into their car, Kite called the Marshton Paper's phone. When Penny Sullivan answered, Kite said, "My name is Sally Whiteside and I have some important information that something really bad is going to happen in Marshton. Can you have the mayor and chief of police meet with me in your office so you can warn the people?"

"What do you mean something bad is going to happen?" Sullivan said in an excited voice.

"I heard my boyfriend talking to his friend and they plan to do something to hurt a lot of people. I'm scared and I want to tell you about it so you can stop them. I can be at your office in less than an hour," Kite said in a scared tone to her voice.

"Are you safe now? Is your boyfriend with you?" Sullivan asked.

"I'm alone now and he is not with me. I will come to your office to tell you what I know," Kite said while faking like she was crying.

"You come to my office and I'll call the mayor and chief of police. Be careful. We'll wait here for you," The editor said trying to sound calm.

"I'll be there as soon as I can," Kite said and ended the call.

"Good job baby. That should have hooked them big time," Willy said.

"Now let's hope she can get the mayor and chief over to her office."

"After your call, I can't see how the mayor and chief can't come. Like I said, you hooked them good," Willy said with a big grin.

"So do we go over there now?" Kite asked.

"Not yet. We give the mayor and chief time to get over there. We want all of our fish to be in the same pond. So we wait a bit," Willy said.

"How do we know that there won't be a lot of other people there?" Kite asked.

"We drive near the paper's office and watch for a spell just to make sure who is going into that office," Willy replied.

Penny Sullivan related to Melissa Travers what she had been told on the phone by a person named Sally Whiteside. Melissa asked, "What kind of harm did she tell you that her boyfriend wanted to do to people?"

"She didn't say, but she sounded scared and I think she was crying," Sullivan said. "Now I have to call the mayor and the chief."

Penny Sullivan called both the mayor and the chief of police and told them both about the phone call she had just gotten and that the woman had said she would be coming to the paper's office as soon as she could get here.

Both the mayor and the chief told Sullivan that they would come right over to the Marshton Paper's office.

Willy and Kite had watched a woman and a man enter the front entrance of the Marshton Paper and Willy said, "That must be the mayor and the chief of police. The fish are in the pond. Time for action."

"So I am going to go in the front door and you will enter from the back door. Don't leave me hanging out in there for long," Kite said.

"You won't be. Walk slow and give me time to drive the car around to the back. Keep the gun covered behind your back and be ready to pull it out as soon as I come into the office.

The Marshton Paper was a large, one story building, with two entrances. It was a fairly old building, with windows on three sides. The building sat alone on a small street that ended at the back of the building's paved parking lot. There was also a parking lot in front.

Kite got out of the car and watched Willy drive around to the back of the building. She then began walking toward the building's entrance.

When Kite walked into the front office, she saw four poeple. Penny Sullivan was standing beside Melissa Travers and Mayor La Clare was seated along with Chief Smithson.

"Are you Sally Whiteside, who called me? Penny Sullivan asked.

Kite didn't answer right away and the four people in the room waited for her to answer. Kite just looked at them and then through a doorway in the rear of the office came Willy holding a pistol aimed in the direction of the shocked four people. Kite also took out her gun from behind her back. The chief pushed call to the first contact on his phone and as he stood up he slid the phone under the stack of ads on the office desk. Neither Willy or Kite saw the move he made with his phone.

Sean, who was still on the patio at Alex's house picked up his phone and heard what sounded like a lot of commotion and yelling. He heard a voice yelling, "Get the fuck down in that chair." Then he heard what sounded like a loud slap and more yelling. He looked at the caller ID and saw that it was the Chief Smithson's phone. Sean quickly pressed the record feature on his phone as he continued to listen. Sean then heard a man's voice say, "All of you assholes get against that far wall. We have a little surprise for the Marshton Paper and you aren't going to like it," Willy said as he picked up the duct tape he brought with him.

"Who are you people?" Sullivan asked.

"We, besides being your worst nightmare, are the people who have been playing games in your woods. We are now going to play some more with you," Willy said as he began to wrap duct tape around the hands of the four people against the far wall.

Sean got up quickly and ran into the house to grab his glock and his car keys. He kept the phone to his ear all the time to listen to what was happening at the location he now knew was that of the Marshton Paper.

Sean also realized that he couldn't call for help or he would lose contact with what was going on in the paper's office. He got into his car and his mind was racing in thoughts of what to do. He drove the short distance to The Marsh bar and ran inside. He saw Cody Wayne at a seat and said, "There is a police emergency and I need you right fucking now. Grab you gun and come with me . . . now!"

Cody Wayne asked, "What emergency?"

"I don't have time to explain. Move it."

Cody could tell that Sean was serious and he got up quickly and went into a side room and came out holding a pistol in his hand. A few other customers in the bar were shocked in silence as Cody and Sean ran out of the bar. "What the hell is going on Sean?" Cody asked as he got into the car.

Sean held the phone up against his ear as he drove out of the bar's parking lot. Sean said to Cody, "Get me the quickest way to the Marshton Paper's location."

At the Marshton Paper, Willy had finished wraping the hands of the four captured people and then began tying Penny Sullivan and Melissa Travers to chairs. Mayor La Clare said in a loud voice, "Why are you doing this to us?"

"Well Mayor Bitch, I'm doing this for revenge for my brother, who was killed by a group of assholes from your town," Willy answered.

"We've been having a good time doing some killing around here. It was fun killing those two troopers in your woods," Kite said as she laughed.

Sean pulled his car short of the paper's building and motioned for Cody to get out. Sean also got out and moved quickly toward the building. Inside the office, Willy made sure the Penny Sullivan and Melissa Travers couldn't move their arms or legs and put duct tape over their mouths. He then laid a pipe bomb under each chair and put duct tape around each bomb.

Sean and Cody reached a side of the building that had windows and looked in to see that Willy was streching out a long fuse that was attached to the bombs under the chairs. Sean saw that both the mayor and the chief had their wrists wraped in duct tape and Kite had just put a piece of duct tape over their mouths. Kite slapped Chief Smithson's face and said, "All cops are pricks."

"We are going to leave you now and take Mayor Bitch and the chief here for a short ride. A very one way ride," Willy said as he bent down to light the fuse that was attached to the pipe bombs.

Sean said to Cody, "Get to the front door and smash it in if you have to. Shoot the lock if you have to but get to that fucking fuse." Cody ran to the front door and Sean moved to the area of the back parking lot.

Willy and Kite were pushing the mayor and the chief out of the back entrance where the car Willy had parked near the back door was parked for the escape.

Cody Wayne slammed into the front door of the building with his shoulder and the door almost caved inwards. He hit it again with his shoulder and the door fell into the office with Cody on top of it. He saw the burning fuse and crawled on hands and knees to reach the fuse when it was only a short distance from the bombs. He pulled on the fuse and crushed the lighted part of the fuse with his hands and took a huge gasp of relief. He felt his forehead where there was a cut.

In the back parking lot Sean raised his glock at Willy and shot him in the head as Willy raised his gun. Kite also raised her gun to shoot at Sean. Chief Smithson pushed Mayor La Clare down and Sean shot Kite between the eyes and her gun went off and the bullet hit the pavement and ricocheted up and hit Sean's forearm. "Shit!" Sean yelled. He then walked over to Willy and kicked the gun from his dead body and did the same to Kite's gun. He then helped Mayor La Clare and Chief Smithson to their feet. Cody Wayne stood at the back door and said, "All is well inside. No bang . . . bang. How is it out here?"

"Some bang . . . bang, but all is mostly well except for another damn ricochet," Sean said smiling through the pain in his arm and then he helped free the mayor and the chief. Mayor La Clare gave a kiss to Sean and to Cody Wayne and thanked each of them for their heroics. Penny Sullivan and Melissa Travers came out to the back parking lot after Cody had freed them and both women hugged Cody for saving their lives.

Chief Smithson said to Sean, "I'm glad you heard my call. Thank you more than I can ever say."

"I recorded everything that went down inside on my phone. It will be a perfect confession by those two," Sean said pointing to the two dead killers.

"I better call Captain Mason and the squad to get rid of those pipe bombs in the office. We sure we lucky you two showed up," He then shook Cody's hand and gave a pat on the back to Sean. "You better get that arm taken care of. I need to get the coroner over here too."

"The arm looks worse than it is. When you call Captain Mason, tell him we got justice for his two murdered troopers," Sean said smiling.

Cody Wayne said to Sean, "Put a bandage on the wound and let's go get a beer or two. I know a perfect place where the beer will be free today."

"Sounds like a good plan to me," Sean said as the fist pumped Cody.

"Sean, before you leave, I normally would have to take your gun and file a shooting incident report, but since I was a witness to the whole deal. I'll pass on the routine matter," Chief Smithson said with a smile.

Cody and Sean got into Sean's car and on the ride back to The Marsh bar Cody said to Sean, "You had a close call in the parking lot with both of those killers holding weapons."

"In a situation like that, if you hesitate, you could end up dead. If you try to just wound someone with a gun that faces you, you could end up dead. I know that's happened to some guys I worked with in the city.

Both of those fuckers that I shot would have killed me and the mayor and the chief. They got what they deserved."

"Well, that was quite the adventure. If someone asked me how my day was? I can say that I smashed a door and disarmed a couple of bombs, but other than that . . . just routine!" Cody said.

"You know you have a cut on your head?" Sean said.

"Yeah well, I'll take the cut rather than what I would look like if those bombs blew."

Sean laughed as he drove into The Marsh parking lot. Both men got out of the car and walked inside the bar. The customers in the bar all turned to look at Cody and Sean. Cody said, "I want a beer for Sean and a bandage and a beer for me."

Judy, the bartender, set two beers on the bar and got a bandage for Cody. Jim Sparta asked Cody," We saw you take off in a hurry. What happened to you two?"

Cody took a long drink of his beer and said, "It sorta was like that World War Two movie, *To Hell and Back*. What do you think Sean?"

"Yes it was or like, a shoot-out at the OK Corral," Sean replied toasting Cody's beer with his.

Hoss asked, "Were you two in a fight?"

Cody answered, "Bombs, bullets and bullshit."

Sean laughed and again toasted Cody's beer with his beer.

Sean then walked away from the bar and texted Alex with the message, "Come to The Marsh bar. I'm in the process of getting loaded for a really good reason." He then walked back to the bar and finished his beer. He ordered a beer for Cody and himself.

Cody pushed his money back and said, "We drink free for as long as we can still stand today because we earned it, that's for sure."

Alex arrived at the bar in thirty minutes and looked at Sean's arm saying, "What in hell happened to you?"

"Get a beer and I'll tell you." Alex got a beer, which Cody said was free for him. Sean then said, "Does the word ricochet mean anything to you?"

Alex looked at Sean's arm and laughed. He then said. "Don't tell me you were in another gun fight and got hit by a ricochet."

"That be the case my friend," Sean said.

Alex listened while Sean did a short recap of what had happened during the day to him and Cody. "You mean the killers were going to blow up the building with the editor and reporter inside and then take the mayor and the chief and kill them too?"

"That appears to be the case. I recorded it all on my phone. Tough day in the town of Marshton, right Cody?"

Cody just laughed and then said to Alex, "You have a friend with a lot of guts Alex."

Sean added, "Cody Wayne is a man with guts, who saved a lot of lives today by getting into that office before any bombs went bang . . . bang. Let's all toast Cody." Everyone in the bar raised a drink in a toast to Cody. Suddenly, through the door walked Captain Mason and Chief Smithson. Both men walked over to Sean and Cody and gave a hug to each man.

Mason then handed the bartender a hundred dollar bill and said, "This is from Darlene La Clare, the mayor. She told me to have you have several rounds of drinks on her." Mason then put the bill on the bar and ordered a drink for everyone in the bar.

The bar was getting quite crowded as word leaked out about what had taken place at the Marshton Paper's office. Chief Smithson told Sean that since the paper's office was a crime scene, that Penny Sullivan and Melissa Travers went to Olean, New York to use the newspaper's machines to print the story that they are going to write. That is why they didn't stop at The Marsh bar.

Ater another hour of celebrating the real closure of the case. Sean and Alex said their goodbyes to all in the bar. Sean shook hands with the chief and Captain Mason, who also were leaving. Sean gave Cody a big hug and slap on the back saying, "Nice doing business with you."

Cody laughed and raised his beer in a toast to Sean and everyone in the bar did the same as Cody did.

Alex and Sean arrived at Alex's house with quite an alcohol buzz on.

Alex built a fire in his pit while Sean called his wife and explained all that took place during the day. Jesse asked him, "Were you hurt at all, during that episode of your's?"

"Just another damn ricochet that just nipped my arm a little. No big deal. No stiches or anything needed much. Beer took care of the pain."

"Sean, are you sure that was all that happened to you?"

"I am sure and I miss you and will be home as soon as the paperwork is done on this case. I'm happy we got justice for the two murdered troopers and for the others killed or injured. Talk to you tomorrow my love. By the way how is your case going?"

"We settled out of court and my client is happy with the settlement and so is my law firm. How long do you think you'll be in Marshton?"

"Just a couple of days to wrap this up with paperwork. I'll call you tomorrow. Alex says hello."

"Tell Alex not to let you get in anymore gun fights."

"I promise not to."

"I love you Sean and I'm glad that it was just another ricochet and not something worse."

"So am I. Talk to you tomorrow. I love you lots." The call ended.

The rest of the night Alex and Sean sat around the fire and talked about all that had happened since that killings started in the Marshton Woods.

EPILOGUE

Penny Sullivan and Melissa Travers worked for several hours on the front page story for tomorrow's paper. The headline for the story read:

HEROIC ACTION SAVES LIVES

The entire front page story recounted the actions by Sean Burns and Cody Wayne and how they, together, brought a final end to the plans of the two people responsible for the killings and other injuries around the town of Marshton. The story told of Cody breaking the paper's door and preventing the bombs from exploding and how Sean had faced the two killers in the back parking lot, who had Mayor La Clare and Chief Smithson hostage, with the intent to murder both of them. Both of the killers were armed and Sean ended both of their lives in a situation that was either him or them who survived. Sean survived and thanks to him so did the mayor and the chief. There were also statements from the mayor and the chief. Penny Sullivan and Melissa Travers also put their feelings in the story about how they were tied to chairs with bombs placed under the chairs set to explode with a lighted fuse. Their story went on to tell all about the terror caused in the woods surrounding Marshton by the two, now dead killers. The front page story ended by again praising Cody Wayne and New York City detective, Sean Burns for their brave actions.

The next morning after Sean had several cups of coffee, he called his captain in New York City and told him of what had transpired at the Marshton Paper's office and that the two people responsible for all of the killings and terror in Marshton had been killed in the parking lot of the paper. The captain asked Sean if he had been injured and Sean told him about the ricochet and his captain laughed and told him to wrap up in Marshton as soon as he could, but take some time to relax. His captain also said that he would contact Isabelle Clarkson and let her know that the real killers were now eliminated and the case was finally closed. He also mentioned that heads were sure to roll at the regional headquarters of the state police, for closing the case too soon. The captain ended the call by telling Sean how proud he was of him and how he had a surprise for him when he returned to the city.

When the call with his captain had ended Sean wondered just what the surprise was that the captain had mentioned?

The word got out to several news outlets and the Marshton Shoot-out became the center of attention by national TV news reports and newspapers. Both Cody Wayne and Sean were interviewed by many reporters in the day following their exploits.

Mayor La Clare set up a special night at Abelli's Restaurant to honor Cody Wayne and Sean Burns. The families of the two murdered troopers were invited to attend the affair and the list of speakers included:

- Mayor La Clare
- Captain Mason
- Chief Smithson
- Isabelle Clarkson
- Penny Sullivan

Cody and Sean were both given special plaques that honored their courage. Carla and George Abelli ordered special New York Strip steaks for the meal as a favor to Sean. Jesse Burns flew back to Marshton on the law firm's plane to attend the event honoring her husband.

When the event ended at Abelli's, Alex, who had brought Jeanene Belloc to the event asked Sean and Jesse to remain at the table for one more drink. When the drinks arrived at the table, Alex said, "I have some good news to share with you, I asked Jeanene to marry me and she said yes!" Alex had a wide smile on his face, as did Jeanene.

Jesse got up to hug Jeanene and Sean stood to give his friend a big hug and a hand shake. Alex then said, "Of course you'll be my best man Sean."

"Your are damn right I will be, you rugby playing professor," Sean said and gave his friend another hug.

"Jesse, how about being my maid of honor?" Jeanene asked.

"I would be honored to," Jesse answered and gave Jeanene a kiss on the cheek.

Sean then asked Carla for a bottle of champagne and Carla brought out a bottle of her best champagne and said, "This is on George and myself for all that you have done."

Sean thanked her and told her that he would always remember Abelli's as a very special place.

Carla then said, "Thank you and stop back if you are ever in Marshton again on a friendly visit and not having to solve a crime."

Sean, Jesse, Alex and Jeanene then finished the champagne and left Abelli's and returned to Alex's house.

At The Marsh bar, Cody Wayne and his friends celebrated Cody's award and being on TV interviews by toasting him several times. Jim and Karen Edwin made Cody another plaque that said,

> To Our Very Own Hero
> Cody Wayne
> We Are Proud of You
> Your Customers

There was a picture of a bear with raised claws on the bottom of the plaque.

The next day Jesse and Sean packed to leave Marshton for New York City. Sean took a phone call from Captain Mason who told him that Carson Thomas was forced to retire from regional headquarters and that Isabelle Clarkson was taking his place. She asked Captain Mason to be her assistant commander and he accepted the position. Sean told him that he deserved the promotion and that he would always be a friend and he also told the captain, that justice never would have happened for his troopers without him continuing the investigation.

Mason thanked Sean for all he had done and also thanked him for turning him on to Harp beer. Sean laughed and ended the call.

Sean and Jesse were packed and ready to leave. Alex and Jeanene told Jesse and Sean that they had planned to marry in June and would look forward to the visit in a few months to the city. They all gave each other hugs and Sean and Jesse left for the airport where Jesse's law firm had sent the plane to take them back to the city.

When Sean finally reported in for work at his headquarters, his captain greeted him and asked him to come into his office. The captain said, "How's that ricochet treating you?"

"Sean answered, "Nothing to it, captain."

"Well, here's the surprise I was telling you about. I am retiring in a month and I am promoting you to take my place as Captain of Detectives. You have earned it in so many ways. It has been approved so all you have to do is say yes."

Sean was shocked and said, "It would be an honor to take the position sir. I will try my best to fill your shoes."

The captain smiled and said to Sean, "You already have in so many ways, but try to lay off those ricochets will you?"

Sean laughed and said, "They are never my intentions."

Both men stood and shook hands.

The End